Two.Gun

The Forgotten Legend of

WILL ADAMS

By William Lee Adams

Cover Painting by Joseph Koerper

TDLAD Publishing
2001 South Valley Drive
Las Cruces, NM 88005
www.tdlad.com

Library of Congress Control Number:
2014944018
Adams, William Lee / Two-Gun

ISBN: 978-0-9817428-1-6 (pbk)

First Edition: September, 2014
Second TDLAD Issue: January, 2015

Printed in USA

0 9 8 7 6 5 4 3

Dedicated to Henry Adams

Who left Somerset, England and arrived in Braintree, Massachusetts in 1638 with wife Edith and a progeny that would come to include multiple nation builders and patriots, two United States Presidents, several United States Congressmen and Ambassadors, and my long line of frontiersmen and cowboys.

Contents

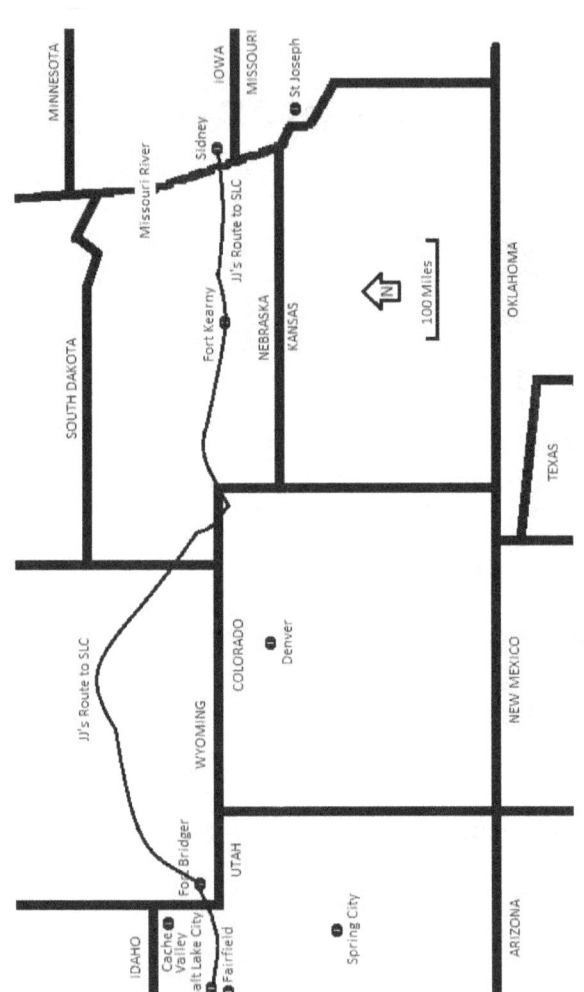

Sidney, Iowa - Salt Lake City, Utah

MAPS

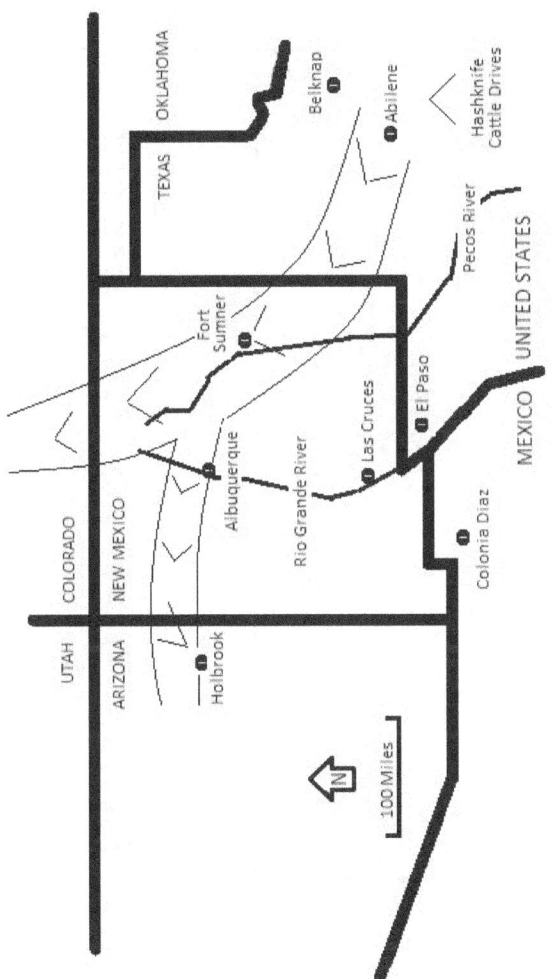

Belknap, Texas - Holbrook, Arizona

MAPS

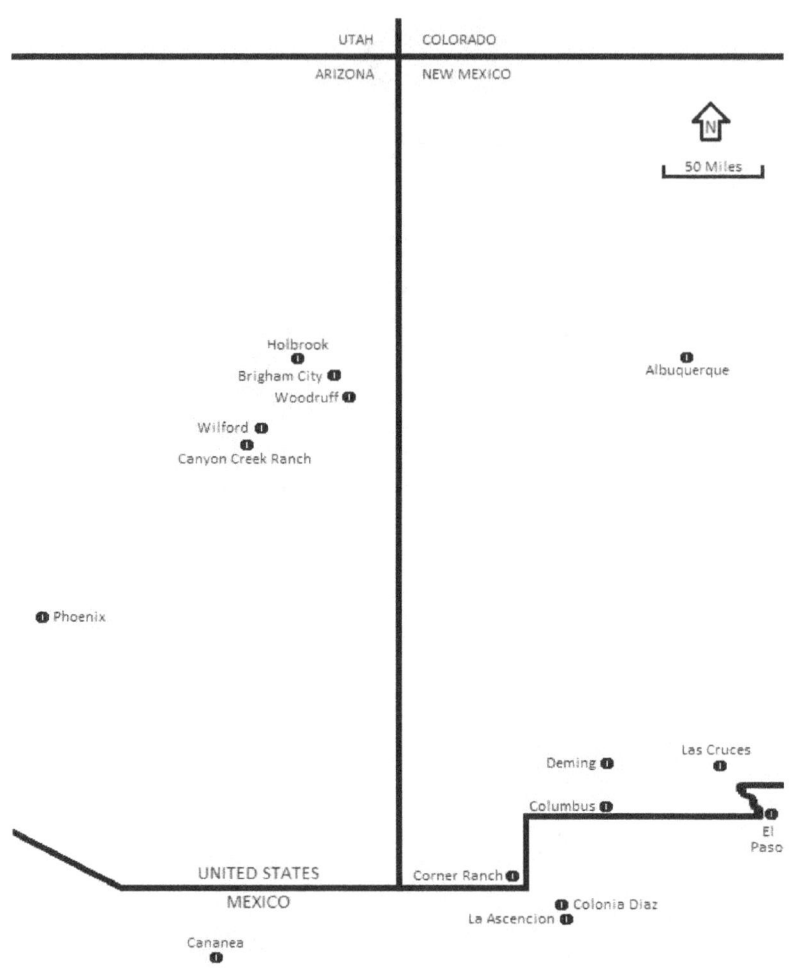

Canyon Creek, Arizona - Colonia Diaz, Mexico

Foreword

I grew up hearing the story of our family. It seemed fantastic – too amazing to be true. Often the story would be told when we gathered around a crackling campfire, tired from a day of deer hunting high in the Black Range mountains of New Mexico, eating our dutch-oven-cooked biscuits, mashed potatoes and pan-fried steaks all smothered with a lake of gravy.

The story had real gunfighters and world champion cowboys, frontiersmen and pioneers – everything a young boy wanted to be when he grew up. That was who my fathers family really was.

It was the story of tragedy turned to instruction - like when my great uncle was accidentally killed by an "unloaded" .22 - which became the foundation for generations learning gun safety.

It was the story of heartbreak as when an entire group of people was forced to evacuate the town they had spent two and a half decades building and flee for their lives.

It was the story of hardship and triumph, of pain and joy. Of incredibly tough people who became even tougher.

This is their (mostly) true story long past time being retold.

Prologue

Colonia Diaz, Chihuahua, Mexico – July 1, 1912

The icy-chill of a mother's certainty that something was very wrong tore at her heart. Although she tried to keep it off her face, she knew it was too late – he had always been able to read her like a book. Concern and worry was written in every blink of his eyes. Those green eyes she adored.

The baby was coming too soon. And it was coming the wrong way. She knew it. At 41, Domer Adams had already given birth to eleven children and knew what to expect. This wasn't it. Always smooth during pregnancy, each birth had also been relatively easy. But this one had been different from the start and was not going smoothly at all.

Still a strikingly handsome, dark-haired beauty, she'd never been able to keep anything from Will, her husband of 24 years.

As she looked at him she was suddenly taken back to when she'd first seen those eyes. She'd been only 12 years old - he was sitting there fully clothed in the middle of that natural pond underneath the huge cottonwood tree in Arizona with a ridiculous grin on his face; as if he'd decided for himself it was the best place to dismount.

Ripples from the shock were still receding when he had turned and looked straight into her, smiling and unconcerned, perhaps a little surprised to find her and the others watching him, but, as always, in command of the situation no matter how funny or serious it might be.

Those same eyes looked at her now, tempered by age. Laugh lines that were evidence of an indomitably cheery outlook in the face of life-long toil and hardship, now were changed to worry about something he could not control.

One hand on her stomach and the other stroking her sweat-damp hair both communicated his concern for her. Against this he could not protect her.

He looked at his mother, Mary, midwife to hundreds of successful deliveries, and saw his worry reflected in her face.

The baby kicked feebly once more - Domer squinted and caught her breath. Feet were in the wrong place, coming first.

Her eyes met his again and in that shared eternal moment they both knew.

Two.Gun

Part I

Iowa – Utah Territory

Sidney, Iowa – March, 1860

The small room was dark and quiet except for the low glow and occasional pop from the dying fire. A blue tendril of flame sneaked out of what remained of the last log from time to time, briefly lighting the face that stared into the open door of the Great Western stove. His wife and sons slept soundly in their beds not far from the radiated warmth while outside more snow piled softly.

The face was strong-featured and full of personality. But eyes that normally twinkled with easy laughter were drawn with care and worry. His 24th winter had been unusually harsh and long-lasting. Rock-hard ground that needed to be turned had languished week after week untouched as the frozen plains of Iowa remained

1

too difficult to work. He worried that seeds not planted would turn into crops not harvested. He thought of his two precious daughters buried in the cold ground outside. His older son was three and the younger barely seven months - would they survive or be taken early too? He didn't think his wife could hold up to the sight of another tiny coffin.

JJ Adams had moved to Sidney with his father William and mother Jane in 1850 from Columbus, Ohio. His father had been looking for open farm land further west, so when JJ was 14 years old the family packed up everything they owned in a small buckboard wagon and set off behind Tony and Jeff, their last two plow horses.

Gold had been discovered in far off California and the itch to move west was in the air. But William was not looking for gold - he wanted soil for growing things and had heard it was to be found on the Iowa plains. The rich and fertile sod, compacted for centuries, never broken or turned by human hand, awaited souls possessed of a hearty constitution.

2

Such a nature was in Boston-born William Jefferson Adams, given him by his progenitors, first landed in America in the 1630's, and in turn passed on to his first son, Jerome Jefferson, who everyone called 'JJ'. Pioneer stock came from JJ's mother too - the Eastwood family name was to be found on the ship's manifest of some of the American Colonies earliest arrivals.

Judge Greenwood and S.T. Cromwell convinced William to stop and stay in their spanking new town of Sidney, insisting they would all become wealthy men by building a stop on the trail west for gold-seekers. So the William Adams family settled just eight miles east of the Missouri river in what became some of the best farm area anywhere in the American plains states.

Two life-changing events happened to the Adams family in August of 1852. On the 18th, the matriarch, Jane, passed away from consumption at age 39. William was devastated as were the three children of which 17 year-old JJ was the oldest. His mother had meant the world to him.

3

Her sudden illness and departure left a hole in his life he thought could never be filled.

But on the last day of that dreary month, the Frost family, on their way west to California from Illinois, stopped and got stuck in Sidney too. JJ would remember the rest of his life the day he first laid eyes on the prettiest girl he had ever seen and fell irreversibly in love. Just ten months later they were married – the only reason they waited that long was because Mary's mother insisted she be at least 17 before she married. They immediately moved onto their own 20 acre table-flat parcel of land not far from both families, built a small home and started their own farm.

William remarried in January of 1853. He had previously known the Wiser family in Ohio and after a brief correspondence, traveled east for a whirlwind courtship of their second daughter, Temperance. When William came back to Iowa with his new bride some semblance of normalcy and stability slowly returned to their home. JJ's new step-mother was kind and selfless to a fault.

While she could never replace his mother, they became immediate and fast friends.

The passing years brought four children to JJ and Mary's little home in Sidney. The first, Rebecca, lived a scant seven months. The second was named for his second cousin, the sixth President of the United States. The third, another daughter, Cora, was exactly eight months old the day she died, leaving behind yet more heartache. Then on September 6th, 1859 a strapping, healthy boy was born. He was named William but called "Will" to avoid confusion with his namesake grandfather.

Will was different than any other baby JJ had ever known. He was physically gifted with coordination far beyond his age. He was a good looking baby too, with a disposition both pleasing and allowing to be pleased. He rarely cried. His mother doted on him, giving to him the affection she would have lavished on her daughters given the chance. But Will remained unspoiled and loving as he grew. In most respects he was the perfect baby – all except the mischief

5

he created. He was into everything as soon as he could crawl at only four months and drove his mother to distraction. When caught doing something he knew he shouldn't, he'd just roll back onto his behind and look up at Mary with a grin that seemed to say "I can't resist!"

St. Joseph, Missouri

Crane Bellows was a hard man in a hard land at a hard time. And it had been a hard winter with snow still on the ground several feet deep in many places and the ground frozen solid.

Outside of the sod-roofed dugout they called their house, he looked at the smoke tendrils rising from the hole he had made in the roof for the round tin pipe that served as a chimney. It drew poorly, so it was always smoky inside when a fire was burning. And a fire was always burning because of the low temperatures for months on end. Crane wondered if this cursed winter would ever be over.

The plains stretched away impossibly far in every direction he looked. His nearest neighbors were three miles away and he had no use for them anyway. He and his boys were on their own.

Their mother had given up her ghost just six months earlier. How such a slip of a woman ever bore him five hardy sons was beyond his understanding. She never had spoken much. Maybe there were some feelings of generosity between them from time to time, but never what one might call love. About the only time she opened her mouth was to nag him about how much whiskey he was drinking.

She never had liked settling there – didn't like the openness after living her early life in the protective mountains of eastern Tennessee. Didn't like the fact they'd moved onto the land just after the first settlers, some no-account Mormons, had been driven out of the state. Now she was planted under that scrawny tree a little too close to the privy. Of her sons, only the youngest, Edge, had seemed to miss her very much. Every once in a while of a cold night

7

Crane Bellows missed her too. He'd never admit it, though.

He stroked his bushy black beard and wondered what to do next. One wagon had a broken axle and the other one wasn't much better. Their last surviving livestock consisted of his horse, one ornery mule and a few scrawny chickens that laid an egg about every other day. Their supplies and food were almost gone and if the weather didn't break soon they'd all starve and join Alice in the Bellows family graveyard.

"Ta hell with this," he muttered to himself, and with a made-up mind went back inside. "Boys, I'm takin' Edge in the good wagon and goin' ta Fort Kearny ta git us some food and what-not. We should be back in a coupla weeks. I want you all ta just stay put until we git back. Anybody comes around giving trouble ya know what ta do."

"But pa, what if something happens to you – how would we ever know?" his eldest son, Able, asked. "Maybe we should all go."

"And have someone move in here and squat on our improvements? Nossir. Besides, it won't take all that long. Able, I know you and Broc has always wanted ta head West, only now's not the time. We got ta git us a stake here, then we kin sell out and all go in better style. Mebbe all the way ta Californy. Look fer some gold."

Broc and Cass exchanged a look that said "I wonder what improvements he's talking about?" The place was in far worse shape than when they got there.

"You boys are full grown and nigh onto men. You kin take care a yer ownsefs if'n ya hafta. I'll hear no snivelin' about it! Able, yer in charge - Broc, don't gimme that look, do what he says. Cass and Dirk, you boys'll hafta pull yer weight too. Take turns doin' yer chores, and if it comes ta no wood y'all chop up and burn that ol' wagon with the busted axle. Take t'other rifle and hunt up some dinner when ya need it. There ain't been nobody yet heard of a Bellows that couldn't do fer himse'f and ya ain't gonna make the first. And

9

careful with that powder and lead, ya hear? It come dear.

"Broc, you and Cass go hitch up Molly. I'll leave the mule here in case ya need 'er. Edge and me'll be 'long directly."

The boys reluctantly traded the warmth of the mud house for the cold barn while Crane wrapped some left over beef from the milk cow they had butchered after it froze to death and the last of the cheese in a neckerchief. He put ten year-old Edge into his heavy coat made of part of a buffalo hide he had traded off a wandering Indian caravan a year earlier. Satisfied the boy was bundled up as good as he was going to get, he nodded to Able and Dirk and stomped out the door with his old Kentucky long rifle wrapped in their bedding, his Colt Dragoon stuck in his belt and their baby brother in tow.

Able and Dirk just looked at each other.

"I guess we might as well fix breakfast. Get some eggs if there is any and I'll start the meat," Able said.

In the barn Crane said "You boys sure is slow. Git a move on. I wanna git ta at least Big Jim's by tonight." He packed their food and bedding in the bed of the wagon and then helped them finish. He double-checked to make sure the harness was tight. "Stop dancin' around and climb up thar, Edge."

Edge, feet already cold, looked horrified by the whole idea of going off into the frozen wasteland but knew better than to backtalk his pa. He climbed up without a word.

"You be good for pa now, Edge," Cass said, sensing his youngest brother's unease. "An' have fun. Bring us back sumthin' sweet from Fort Kearny!"

Crane slapped the reins to the back of Molly - the wagon rolled a few inches after a lurch and then settled back. "You boys take care a each other – we'll be back in about two weeks or not at all. Hyah! Hike it, Molly!"

Able and Dirk had come outside to watch. Cass waved to Edge who waved back just as the wagon topped out and went down into Squaw

Creek and was lost to sight. All four boys looked a little shocked that they were suddenly alone. Silently they went back into the dugout and shut the door against the cold.

◆

The Mormons were a problem. Everybody knew it. Even though they had been driven out of Missouri and Illinois, after Joe Smith and his brother had been killed at Carthage in 1844, and were now settled in the Great Basin of the Salt Lake Valley, they were still very much on the minds of people all over the United States.

That's because in 1852 polygamy had been publicly declared as being practiced by the "Saints", as they called themselves, in the two year old Utah territory. What's worse, it had been going on for years with very few people even inside the church knowing. For some time since the announcement the country had been up in arms about what to do with the scandalous

Mormons who now wanted to join the union as a state. It had even been reported in the New York Times that Territorial Governor Brigham Young himself was married to more than 20 wives!

JJ could not imagine why those women put up with it. Or why any God-fearing person would tolerate it, for that matter. Something should be done and it all seemed to be Brigham Young's fault. Anyone living such an immoral life ought to be hanged. That's all there was to it.

"What are ya thinking about?" Mary asked as she gathered her blanket around her and sat beside her husband.

Momentarily startled, JJ continued to stare into the stove.

"Oh, ah dunno. Ah guess ah was jes thinkin' on mebbe we might wanna move further west. This infernal winter jes won' stop. Ah don' wanna drag ya away from yer folks, but we can' go on like this. We'll be starvin' long before this time next year if'n we can' get crops in the ground soon."

13

"We'll manage. We have so far. An' I'm not the only one'll be leaving folks if we move on. What about your pa an' step-ma?"

JJ had been considering this very thing. "Ah been thinkin' they kin have our farm here. That'll give 'em 'nother 20 acres an' mebbe find someone they kin rent it out to. Ah'm not so sure ah'm cut out ta be a farmer, anyhow."

"Sounds like ya got it all worked out, huh? An' when were ya gonna talk ta me 'bout this?" she needled him with a grin and a poke in the ribs.

He looked at her with a smile. "No matter what, ah'm the luckiest man around ta have ya with me. Ever since that first day ah saw ya, ah knew it." He chuckled and pulled her close to him.

"Aw, JJ, ya know I'll go where ya wanna go an' do what ya do. But ya really think it's a good idea ta leave now, with all the snow an' ice an' cold still with us? Will's only seven months old, 'member."

"That boy'll be jes fine." He winced at his hasty words when he saw Mary's face turn

14

suddenly cold with eyes far away. He knew she was thinking of their lost baby girls.

"He's strong an' ya know how determined he is. John Q also. 'Sides, it'll be harder once the thaw comes. This country'll turn ta pure-d-mud a foot'r more deep. Won't be much fun a-tall sloggin' through when that happens."

She came back from her reverie with a sigh. "Yer right, I know it. I'm jes a worry wort." She laughed a little to help drive away the demons.

JJ took her more tightly into his arms; they shared the blanket and each other's warmth.

"No yer not. An' yer right ta worry. Keeps muh crazy idears in check, sometimes. But still, ah do think this'll be best. Ah heerd tell in Californy miners an' even normal folk be need'n meat. Ya think ah could raise up some cows out thar?" He smiled at her.

She smiled back. "JJ, I do believe you kin do whatever comes ta that mind a-yers."

◆

The wagon creaked and complained like an old woman as Crane coaxed it over the bleak, frozen trail. At first Edge's toes felt like they were going to fall off despite being buried in two layers of thick socks and worn-out boots. Now they were pretty much numb. He wondered if he ought to be worried he couldn't feel them, but didn't want to ask his pa. Pa didn't go for a lot of talk anyway, and he didn't look to be in the mood today to change the tradition.

Big Jim's was a few miles behind them. Crane had spent the best part of the night drinking with Jim and then snored for a few hours before staggering out to the wagon with Edge nervously following behind.

Jim himself had come from the rougher part of Irish Boston, but made it no further than the tiny "trading post" he had thrown together out of whatever scraps of lumber he could find at the time. Word was Jim wasn't his real name and had escaped his previous environs a jump ahead of two giant brothers who didn't like seeing their baby sister beat up.

He was a big man - the name Jim was the first thing that had come to mind, so Big Jim it was. Quite a few folks on the frontier didn't go by the name they were born under.

Really no more than a place to get out of the cold and drink the rot-gut Jim made himself, it had become a hangout for some of the crustier characters in the area and on the trail west. Crane Bellows fit that description.

Jim didn't have any trade goods this time of year, especially with the way the weather had been. Not only was no resupply coming any time soon, but Jim had long been cleaned out of what meager stocks he had, except the items carefully squirreled away for his own use.

It was still better than 150 miles to Fort Kearny. Crane figured he might have gone back east a ways or even right in St. Jo's to find most of the things they needed, but he was feeling the itch to get out and see some country. Kearny was a supply fort which would have news of what was going on. Plus, the soiled doves were much more

17

plentiful around an army fort than they were in St. Jo's.

There was another reason he had decided to go all the way to Kearny – it was a stop for the growing traffic of the Oregon Trail. Lots of pilgrims and other tenderfeet passed over that road on their way west. Without enough money to buy all the things they needed his only recourse would be to take some. Crane knew somewhere along the trail folks could be coaxed into helping him out. He wouldn't take everything they had - he did have *some* scruples, after all. That's how he thought of it in his own mind, justifications being so handy to Crane he didn't have any bad ideas lacking at least one.

Having Edge along just gave him some company - he didn't worry what he might be teaching the boy by example. It was a hard life and, if anything, he could pass along the idea that sometimes you had to take what you needed. Nobody was just giving it away. The boy was ten years old - now was as good a time as any to learn

18

the way of things. He could use some toughening up.

♦

Their emotional goodbyes said to the Frosts the previous evening and last hugs exchanged, Mary and the two boys were seated in the wagon, ready to move west. The weather was awful – low rolling clouds of gray promised more snow, more wet and more bitter cold. JJ was almost convinced putting off their departure for a day or two might be best as his father suggested.

Neither his nor Mary's parents had been very happy about their plans to move to California. They would miss their children and grand-children, but William more than anyone understood the urge to move on to something better. Even though he would spend the rest of his life in Iowa and Ohio, he too had keenly felt the pull of the west.

19

"You sure you wanna leave in this? It might just turn ta blizzard an' you don't wanna be caught up in that out on the flat." William and JJ were off a ways talking.

"Pa, ah've got a feelin' this'll let up purty soon. An' 'sides, if'n we stay too long we'll end up bogged down once the ground thaws. Mary's put in enough blankets an' quilts ta keep a whole injun tribe warm an' ah can' even see li'l Will fer all the bundlin' up he's got on."

JJ's family sat in the three-by-eleven wagon with all their belongings in the world, watching him and his father, ready to go. Everyone knew it was time - they all hesitated to face it.

"An' you got that gun loaded an' ready ta hand?" William asked his son. He had given JJ his almost new Remington New Army revolver with an extra cylinder for protection on their trip west. JJ also had an older muzzle-loading rifle he'd be using to hunt fresh meat wrapped in a quilt.

"Yessir, ah do an' the other cylinder too. Ah cast plenty a lead fer both a them guns an' ah got the powder whar it won't git wet an' a bunch a caps too. Ah thankee, pa, fer lettin' us have that. Ah'm shore it'll come handy."

"You'll need it more'n us an' I'll get another one come spring. Well, boy, I guess this's it. You all take good care an' send word when you light somewhere's. We might jes be followin' one a these first days, you never can tell. Temperance's got that itchy foot," he winked. JJ's step-mother had joined them.

"Ya old liar. Don't ye be tellin' your son such right when's they be leaving, William Jefferson Adams. He be know'n full well who's the foot what itches an' brought first ye an' then me here, a'ready." She never let her husband get the best of her. "An' I be thinkin' he inherited that foot a-ye's."

The men grinned at each other and then turned serious, the import of the moment heavy in the air. They shook hands and looked away quickly, lest the knowing this might be the last time they saw each other show in their eyes. JJ hugged his step-mother tightly and trudged to the wagon

21

where his family waited. He looked one last time at their tiny home close by the small crosses marking the graves of their two infant daughters. His breath caught at the sight, but he climbed up beside his wife, taking the reins resolutely into his gloved hands.

Silently, William and Temperance watched as heavy flakes of snow began to fall softly. JJ marveled that they seemed so stoic – Temperance was a deceptively strong woman. He nodded to them both and with a click of his tongue started the two oxen and wagon.

Slowly they rolled out of sight. Waving hand dropping to her side, no longer needing to be strong for JJ, who she considered her son, she finally broke, tears running freely down her cheeks. "I'm thinkin' I'll no be seein' my boy or my sweet gran-chillen ag'in." Her premonition proved correct – neither of them ever traveled further west than where they then stood.

William held her thin, wiry body tightly, his own eyes almost spilling over. "Come on, doll," he said raggedly. "Let's get ya outa this cold."

He gently helped her into their own wagon, climbed up beside her, and old Jeff rattled them off in the opposite direction.

◆

A day ahead, the morning dawned bright and crisp. The snow had stopped and the clouds fled in the last few hours of the night, leaving a vivid orange in the east as the sun commenced its daily journey. Tiny points of fragile crystals reflected the infinite morning light.

That beauty was lost on Crane - the morning brightness only made him squint with a sour expression. They had made a wet and miserable camp the evening before, using as many blankets as they could against the night. Their make-shift tent under the wagon had kept most of the snow off, but it piled on each side as it fell. Every time Crane wiggled the snow and cold seemed to move in with him. The sodden blankets held little warmth and the equally wet wood he pulled from

23

beneath the new snow made for a small and struggling fire.

Coffee finally on the boil and bacon sizzling in the skillet raised his spirits a little. The sun gave increasing warmth as it climbed. He figured they would raise Fort Kearny this day - by his reckoning they had to be within 10 miles or so, although the stark, unchanging landscape made it just a guess.

"Git up outa that bed, Edge. You need ta shake a leg so's we kin git goin'."

Being under the middle of the wagon kept him much cozier than his father and he had spent a relatively nice night sleeping soundly. The out-of-doors takes less a toll on youth. He didn't feel a bit like leaving his warm bed, but didn't relish the kick in the ribs he might get if he didn't.

They had seen no one on the trail since leaving Jim's place. No tracks in the snow. No evidence anyone or thing had passed this way for a great while. It was like they were the last people on earth. The dismal plains went on as far as they

24

could see, broken only by copses of trees scattered here and there.

Crane realized he should have known the easy pickings would stay indoors where they were comfortable until spring had finally started chasing away the dregs of winter. He had purposely been going slowly, both because of the condition of the wagon and so any early pilgrims might overtake them.

No sooner had these thoughts finished crossing his mind than did a lone wagon bump its way out of a distant roll behind them. It was on the trail, headed in their direction. Crane fingered his Colt, thinking his luck had finally changed.

It had.

"Edge, jes stay put right whar y'are. Don' move an' don' say a word."

◆

JJ and family made their way up the faint, snow-covered track. The passing Nebraska landscape left them without knowing quite where they were since everything looked the same out there. The low rolling prairie glistened white in the bright sun everywhere they looked. The wagon gave them a rough ride, but it was better than walking in the snow where feet could freeze in short order, toes first.

So far the boys and Mary had done just fine out under the expansive sky with no complaints. JJ was himself thinking about just how uncomfortable it was to move around out here, but it was even worse when they stopped. Until a decent fire could be started to chase away the pervasive cold it penetrated to the bone. Simple tasks became more difficult and demanded concentration. In their beds at night it always seemed frigid no matter how many blankets they used.

Still, JJ mused, it was better that the ground was frozen for their purposes. The two oxen were just enough to pull the size of wagon they needed to hold their provisions. The extra resistance of a melting roadway with its attendant mud would imperil their journey and require them to get off and help the team betimes.

He felt better than ever about their decision to move west. Even though the way was difficult, ultimately he was sure they'd be better off in California. All his life he'd only known hard winters and was looking forward to being where it was warm. He knew Mary felt the same - it was one of the reasons she so readily agreed to the abrupt move, although she wasn't so keen on his idea to hang Brigham Young along the way.

How would he even do such a thing, he wondered? The more he thought about it, the more his anger cooled at the man he thought was responsible for polygamy.

Their way west led straight through Salt Lake City so he figured he'd wait and see what happened. He felt as if he was being urged forward with something specific for him to do. He'd gotten that feeling several months back, just after Will was born. He couldn't explain it – it was simply something he had to act on.

He had seen a man hung once. Shortly after they had arrived in Sidney, a popular family by the name of Rogers had been killed further south in Missouri. No one ever quite knew for sure who did it, but the grisly nature of the crime – a little girl and tiny baby boy had been murdered, along with their parents, but not until even worse things were done to the mother – concentrated the entire area into action.

A man named Ike Darrel McCaskill was discovered living alone on the small Rogers farm. When questioned he said he knew nothing about anyone there – he had just happened upon the apparently abandoned homestead, moved in and made himself at home. The entire Rogers family was found thinly covered in a shallow hole only a hundred feet or so from the tiny house. Decay had set in; the scene was gruesome.

McCaskill tried to throw suspicion on Indians he claimed to have seen in the area, but Indians didn't normally bury their own dead and certainly wouldn't have cared about a white family. Eventually McCaskill admitted that he had buried them all by himself and cleaned the place up, but that they were already dead when he arrived.

Emotions ran high and hot - the trial in the small structure normally used for school packed in spectators from all around. By defending himself McCaskill sealed his fate and was convicted of the crime in less than an hour by a jury of seven local men. Circuit Judge Kevin Wilton sentenced him to death by hanging.

It took only a day for a gallows to be constructed, but in that short time word spread like prairie fire. Hangings were much more common in Texas, but to the local country it was a rare spectacle. William Adams decided to take his family to see the proceedings and get supplies at the same time. JJ never had forgotten the pitiful image of the crying man's face when the hangman put a burlap bag over it.

Since relatively few local people had any experience with hanging, the distance of the fall

29

needed to break a neck had been over-estimated. JJ and many another soul that day would never forget the unique and awful sound of a man's head being ripped from his body. Women fainted dead away while others screamed and cried; even hardened men turned their heads as the body convulsed and bled by the bucket-full.

Though few believed Ike McCaskill was not guilty of the crime, his grisly death made some think twice about brutal frontier justice. Still, there was the poor Rogers family to remember, and that justice, if not necessarily clean, was at least quickly dispensed.

JJ shuddered involuntarily as he thought back on it. Mary looked over at him.

"Doin' alright, honey?"

"Yep. Jes thinkin' 'bout thangs a bit."

"It's an awful way ta die." She knew her man well.

He glanced at her and laughed. "Woman, sometimes ah think yer some kinda witch!"

"All a us got some part witch in 'em, I s'pose." She winked. "But it ain't hard guessin' what's on yer mind. I can't imagine what it was like seein' that head rollin' around on the ground. I don't think I'll live long enough ta ever wanna witness such a thing myself."

"Well, ah shore been thinkin' on it, an' ah got no idear how things'll go when we git ta Salt Lake City. Ah do know ah need ta see it through, one way or t'other. That thar polygamy jes ain't right. Someone has gotta stand up ta 'em an' ah guess that someone is gonna be me."

"Yer right about that. I could never share ya with another woman. I'm 'fraid I'd be smilin' at'er one minute an' tearin' 'er eyes out the next!" she smiled sweetly at him.

JJ chuckled. "Yup. Yer most certainly not the kind ta take that nonsense from no-one."

The wagon rolled along uneasily over unforgiving ground. They sat lost in their own thoughts as the country passed them by going the other way. Mary rested her eyes from the glare and pictured the boys.

John Q was the most interested of the family. He couldn't seem to get enough of the subtle changes in the vista. He was a quiet boy, but very intelligent with his mother's facial features and dark eyes.

Will, on the other hand, was still as precocious as ever. He didn't like being cooped up in a swarm of blankets and was opposed to being held for too long. Under Mary's watchful eye he'd been allowed to crawl around in the back of the wagon with John Q as well as he could amongst their belongings. He couldn't really move much, but it gave him time to do for himself. When he would get on his knees to pull his little head above short sides to peek over she'd have to put her foot down. She'd pull him back only to see him right back up there a few seconds later. She couldn't get mad at him, though - he always had the biggest smile on his face for her.

Mary came awake with a start. The constant rocking motion of the wagon had lulled her into dozing, but that had changed abruptly when the rocking stopped. She looked at JJ and found he was tense and concentrating ahead of them; the Remington revolver lay in his lap.

32

The object that drew his attention was another wagon, dusted with new snow, just enough off the beaten track at an angle to make it look odd. Nothing moved – no one seemed to be nearby, but something felt wrong.

"Stay here," was all he said, getting down carefully and cocking the gun. Suspecting a trick, he advanced slowly, expecting at any moment to be waylaid. His trigger finger felt clumsy in his glove. He took it off and stuffed it in his coat pocket.

The wagon was empty save for a few blankets strewn in the back. There were no fresh tracks, but the ground around had been dug up by horses hooves and then refrozen along with some wagon tracks. The remnants of a fire made him look around again carefully - what looked like dark paint had dripped over the edge of a flat rock and frozen into mini stalactites. He knew it wasn't paint. Squatting, he saw where there seemed to be two parallel lines trailing off over a small rise along with some boot tracks. Light snow had fallen since this happened.

Looking back at his own wagon he saw John Q and Mary watching him intently, she holding Will. He motioned for them to stay where they were, deciding he'd better follow the tracks. This close to Fort Kearny he figured against it being Indians. Plus, they didn't drag their victims away from the scene of a slaughter.

Muzzle first, still suspecting ambush, he grimly followed the trail to what he was sure he didn't want to see, and yet wasn't prepared for what he found.

Crane Bellows stared straight at him, sitting wide-eyed and teeth gritted, back to the side of a dry rivulet with a grimace on his face that would have given pause to the devil himself. Not only dead, but frozen in place, his eye lashes and brows and beard frosted. JJ shivered, but not from the cold. The round hole in his forehead was only the final wound - it looked like he'd been shot several more times in the body.

Frozen next to him was what appeared to be a young boy maybe eight to ten years old. He looked like he could be sleeping, bundled from head to toe, only his small face peeking out.

Damn, he thought, *what in* hell *happened here?*

He was glad he was where Mary and John Q couldn't see this. The tragic scene was obviously a day or so old - it was amazing wolves or some other predator hadn't gotten to the bodies yet. Then he noticed the boy had a huge revolver in his lap.

Suddenly he had more questions than answers. What to do with the bodies? Even if he could move them back to his wagon he wasn't sure he should, and he didn't really have any place to put them. Besides, he didn't want Mary and the boys riding with the frozen bodies the rest of the way to Fort Kearny.

He'd report it, of course, and the army would probably send someone to investigate, so he didn't want to disturb the area. He wasn't sure what the local civilian authority was here.

Whatever animal had been pulling the poor man's wagon was gone. He looked to have been robbed and killed. Maybe the child had hidden somewhere and then fought off whoever did this with his father's gun until he had succumbed to the cold.

Burying the two strangers was also out since the ground was still solid. Besides, he didn't think he should be tampering with the scene at all - even his own tracks would confuse things enough.

He decided they'd just have to stay there until he could get someone from the fort to come out to take care of it and do whatever investigating they needed to. Fortunately, they weren't far from that help.

He started to walk back, the snow crunching under his boots. But something made him turn to look again - the boy's eyes were now open and staring straight at him. *What the...?*

As JJ moved closer the boy tried to raise the big gun.

"Ah mean ya no harm, son. Ah'm here ta he'p. Come on now, les git ya up outa thar." JJ had nothing to fear for the boy obviously didn't have

36

remaining strength enough to lift the gun, much less shoot it.

"This's some tough kid," he thought. How had he ever survived the freezing temperatures out here by himself?

JJ rotated the cylinder of his own gun back to the empty chamber, let the hammer down and settled it in his belt. He put his glove on before stooping to pick the boy up and carrying him whole in his blankets back to the wagon. Even with all his clothes and gun it didn't feel like he weighed much more than a 50 pound sack of flour.

Mary placed Will in John Q's arms and jumped down to meet them.

"Got a ver' cold boy here. Need ta git 'im warmed up right away an' git some hot food into 'im."

"Here, ya give him ta me an' git a fire goin'." Edge stared at her with big somber eyes, as if worried by blinking she might disappear.

37

JJ gently took the big Colt from the boy. He checked the loads and finding none left set it in the wagon floor board.

As JJ started a fire, she rocked him gently and tried to give him as much warmth as she could. He never took his eyes off her.

"What's yer name, son?" she asked. "Where have ya come from? Can ya say what happened here? Where's yer folks?" The flurry of questions brought no response.

JJ caught her eye, giving her a little shake of his head. Mary took that to mean they must be dead somewhere close.

"Oh my lands. Well, yer safe now an' you kin tell us yer name later on once ya've thawed out an' had sumthin' ta eat. Are ya hungry?" Edge still said nothing, just looked into her face. "I bet ya are. I think we're goin' ta have an early lunch right here." She smiled at him hoping it would make him feel better.

Mary made some beef broth for the boy. At first she couldn't get him to eat at all. Reluctantly, he slowly allowed some to warm his mouth.

38

After a few spoonfuls he ate eagerly and drained several bowls.

JJ gave him some cheese and bread which also disappeared quickly. "Ya take it jes a lil more slowly thar, boy. We'll move on when ya feel up ta it. What's yer name?"

Edge stared at him, chewing in silence.

"Well, son, ah know ya been through a wringer. Ya jes tell us when yer good an' ready, then."

Off to one side him and Mary consulted in low tones:

"Are his folks over yonder?"

"One of 'em is. His pa, ah reckon. Din't see nobody else. How that boy survived out here by hisself is beyond my knowin'. Looks like he fought off whoever kil't his pa an' they jes left him out here ta freeze. Onny he din't. Ah'll report that wagon abandoned when we git ta Fort Kearny an' they kin send someone out here ta git it an' investigate."

"What'd ya see over thar, JJ? Yore still 'bout as white as new snow."

"Nothin' good an' nothin' we kin do anythin' 'bout. We jes need ta get on in ta Kearny an' let the proper 'thorities know what's out here."

Mary decided not to press her husband. He doused the fire while she gathered everything back into the wagon. She put the boys in the bed and sat the new boy between her and JJ.

The wagon started with a jerk and they rolled slowly by the abandoned one. Elements had combined to begin covering it up. Nothing lasted long without constant guard out there.

Edge stared straight ahead.

Fort Kearny, Nebraska - April, 1860

Calling it a "fort" was being generous, JJ thought. Although it did have some earthen works thrown up, it looked more like a frontier town than a fort. It had no outer walls for defensive purposes, only a bunch of mud buildings and a very few wooden frame structures. Indeed, the army used it mainly as a supply point and depot.

As one of the first major stops on the route of the brand new Pony Express, which ran from St. Joseph to Sacramento, mostly along the Oregon and California trails, the fort that honored General Stephen Watts Kearny was a frontier outpost in a central location. In later years the town of Kearney would grow up close by where Fort Kearny had been, the renegade "e" added by the infallible United States Post Office and never after corrected.

For the U.S. Army it would come to be a vital supply point in the Indian wars still years ahead, even though the fort itself would never see hostilities. Soldiers from the fort would often accompany wagon trains on their way west and refugees from Indian attacks could seek the relative safety it provided.

Major John Spader was in command. That a lowly major was the ranking officer said a lot about the mission and purpose the fort served at that time.

41

Smoke curled lazily from several stovepipes as JJ and family rolled to the wide veranda that fronted the largest of the mud-walled structures. He got down from the wagon and stepped up onto the covered porch. The street looked almost deserted with the exception of a few soldiers on duty. They barely gave him a glance. He pushed the door open and went inside.

A lone officer was sitting behind a large desk scribbling in a ledger book. He didn't look up. JJ waited, hat in hand for the officer to finish. After a few minutes he cleared his throat.

"I'll be with you momentarily." Again without looking up from his work.

Finally, he finished writing, sanded the page and closed the book. "How can I help you, sir?"

"Ah need ta report a murder."

"I see. Who has been murdered?" He asked matter-of-factly, opening a different book.

"Well, ah'm not rightly sure. We, muh fam'ly an' me, come upon an abandoned wagon a few miles out east a town. Ah looked 'round a lil an' found a man had been shot an' drug off with his lil boy."

"So there have been two murders."

"No," JJ said. "Jes the father was dead. We've got the boy with us - we brung him in. The tyke hasn't said a word yet. Musta been through hell an' back."

"Just a moment while I talk to the Major. Can you bring the boy in here?"

"Mayn't ah fetch in muh fam'ly too? It's warm in here."

"Certainly, sir. You may bring them all in if you like. I'll be back shortly."

JJ went outside to his family who were cold and restless in the wagon. "Army man says ta come on in. Here, gimme Will an' you bring the other two." Mary handed him to JJ, then climbed down herself and picked up John Q and set him on the porch.

"Come on, little one. We're gonna go inside whar it's warm."

Edge looked at her uncertainly, then jumped off the wagon to follow her.

43

Just after they situated themselves by the stove the inner door opened again and the officer came out accompanied by an older man also in uniform.

"I'm told you found a dead man outside the fort and brought in a young boy as well. My name is Major Spader and I'm in command here. May I ask what your name is, sir?"

"Ah'm Jerome Adams an' this's muh wife, Mary, an' our two lil boys. This'n here is the boy we found sittin' by the dead man. Ah fig'red it ta be his pa."

Edge's whole body had stiffened at the sight of the two Army officers. He looked at their uniforms with wide eyes and clearly an expression close to terror.

Major Spader dropped to a knee in front of the boy. "You have nothing to fear here, young man. What is your name?"

No response.

"He hasn't said a word, Major," Mary offered from across the room. "We guessed he's really been through something awful an' lost his voice fer now."

"Yes, ma'am. I think you're right about that. But we'll need to know who he is and where he comes from if we are to get in touch with his relatives - if he has any."

Leaving John Q to hold Will, Mary came over to Edge, kneeling in front of him. "Son, can ya tell these Army men who y'are an' where ya come from? It's ok, they're tryin' ta help ya."

Edge shook his head violently. Silent tears rolled down his cheeks. He threw his arms around her neck, his little shoulders heaving.

"Ah'm not rightly shore what ta do," JJ said, scratching his head. "He jes 'bout won't git outa sight a muh wife. Mebbe has a touch a brain fever. Ah shudder ta think what he mighta saw out yonder."

"I think we can finish taking this man's statement, Lieutenant. Get Sergeant Wright in here on the double to lead a squad back up the road to recover the body."

"Thar's a wagon out thar too, sir."

"Instruct the sergeant to take whatever he thinks necessary to bring back the wagon and the dead man, then. Tell him to keep his eyes open so he can report back."

"Yessir," said the Lieutenant.

"Mr. Adams, when you get done giving your statement I'd like to talk privately to you in my office, if I could."

JJ nodded.

◆

"Come in and set yourself down, Mr. Adams. Make yourself comfortable. I've got a problem."

JJ sat in a high-backed wooden chair. Major Spader's office was homey but sparse.

"We're getting more and more of this type of thing. Orphans and widows are not something we're prepared to deal with here. If we can't get any information from the boy there's no way we can notify his relatives. Do you have any ideas?" He looked pointedly at JJ.

46

JJ squirmed in his chair. "Well, no sir, ah don't know what kin be done. Ain't thar someone aroun' could take 'im in 'til he kin talk ag'in?"

"That's just it. All the men here, including myself, are single. The only women around are not quite the motherly type, if you take my meaning. In a month or perhaps even a few weeks we'll have wagon trains in here almost every day, but with this cold you're just about the first we've seen moving so early."

"Ah understan' yer meanin'. What do ya plan on doin' with the boy, then?"

The major shifted in his chair. "Where are you headed, if you don't mind my asking?"

JJ wasn't sure he liked the sound of where this was going. "We're goin' ta Californy ta raise beef cattle," he said guardedly. He wasn't about to tell Spader his idea for when he stopped in Salt Lake City.

"Listen, Mr. Adams, I'll not beat around the bush. Do you think you could take the boy with you? You'd be taking in what appears to be an orphan and doing the Army a big favor. You've a

47

young family and it's obvious the boy will be terrified of your wife leaving without him."

"Well, now Major, ah won't say ah hadn't thought a it a'ready, bein' the Christian thing ta do, but ah've not spoken of it ta muh wife. It's also another mouth ta feed. An' what if thar's folks a his lookin' fer 'im? Ah'd not want ta keep 'im from his fam'ly jes from not knowin' who they are."

The Major thought for a moment. "Yes, I see what you mean. Here's what we could do: if you and your wife will consent to take him along with you, I will give you an Army chit for the extra foodstuffs you may require. Additionally, if the boy ever tells you who he is, you can contact me here and I'll use my influence to find any relatives he may have and let them know where he is. Will that be acceptable?"

"Ah 'spose so. But ah'll still need ta talk it over with the missus first."

"Of course. Mr. Adams, you'll be doing the Army and the boy a big favor. Please talk with your wife then let me know what you decide."

◆

"Oh, JJ! He needs us! Have ya thought that maybe the reason ya kept feelin' the need ta get goin' early was because we were bein' led right to 'im? How could we abandon 'im now?"

JJ cautioned her, "It might jes be fer a lil while, anyhow. If'n he tells us who he is the Major says he'll find his relatives an' let 'em know whar he's at." He marveled at his wife. Not a moment of hesitation about taking in a boy they had never seen before that morning.

"I've got a feeling his ma might be out there somewhere's dead. Think about it. His pa killed an' him left ta freeze. I think whoever did it may have dragged his ma off with 'em. But no matter what happened, we kin take care of 'im until an' if relatives are found that kin take 'im in. 'Til then, we gotta be his ma an' pa," she said.

JJ sighed. "Ah know yer right. It's the onny thing we kin do. Ah'll tell the Major."

49

◆

So it came to be the first light saw the Adams wagon leave Fort Kearny behind with two additions: a ten year-old boy and a two year-old horse. JJ had planned to buy the latter which instead came courtesy of the U.S. Army.

It would be almost two years before Edge spoke a word to his new family. By then he was far from any blood relatives - Able and Broc fighting for the Confederacy at little-known places with names that would become household words; Cass and Dirk still back in Missouri trying to improve the family farm.

Might we condense? Thank you. Not that their other adventures on the Oregon Trail weren't noteworthy, but our story lies elsewhere.

Fortune rose and fell in turn for the Adams clan as they moved west – wheels broke, oxen mired, food shortaged, rivers raged, natives threatened – trials deepened. But someone neglected telling those intrepid souls the way was easy so they all forgot to complain.

Through Nebraska they went and into Wyoming. Mountains sprang up to give the journey variety. A left turn off the Oregon trail near Independence Rock yielded Fort Bridger and the beginning of the California leg. Thence, straight over the line into the Utah Territory, finally led the hardy travelers to a new city in the mountains next to a dead lake having the sun for its only outlet.

Salt Lake City, Utah Territory - July, 1860

In a room off his residence at the Beehive house, which served as his main office, Brigham Young sat at his desk deep in thought. The new Seth Thomas regulator clock chimed once claiming 4:30am. As always, the affairs of the church and people he led weighed heavily on his mind.

He didn't sleep well – he couldn't remember the last morning he wasn't the first one out of bed. He knew some people thought he was severe, but it hadn't always been that way. He recalled much of his youth spent in mirth and sighed wistfully for times that could never come again.

He'd just turned 59 years old. He and his people were increasingly threatened by a government they'd first asked redress of and then fled from in order to practice their religion as they saw fit. But their Rocky Mountain refuge was fast becoming less remote.

In part it was due to their own success. Ever industrious, like the residents of the symbolic sculpture atop his home, the Mormons routinely worked like bees and the fruits of their labors made for a blossoming section of North America talked about throughout the nation they'd left behind to seek religious freedom. It also became a beacon on a hill - attracting immigrants from the old countries in Europe.

Their missionary labors as a church were a double-edged sword that cut both beneficial - as

52

those converts poured in - and challenging since most of the people were very poor and needed to be taken care of initially. Until they could get on their feet the church storehouses were hard pressed to keep up.

He felt responsible for each and every one of them.

He sat back and by flickering lamp light opened his scriptures to read about an earlier people who settled in harsh lands and prospered while they remembered their God and were righteous. His glasses slipped off his nose and into his lap.

People were going somewhere. They packed belongings onto the backs of mules in strange looking woven baskets. Children ran beneath parents feet – playing festively as they always do while their grown-ups went about their preparations.

These were completed without words; the hushed group of people in drab coats rounded up young ones and the company started. Laden mules trudged slowly off into tentacles of mist

53

that seeped out of the ground. Hand drawn carts with big wooden wheels, equally full, followed behind pulled by men with no faces. No one looked at him as the procession walked by, but he got the sense he was the reason they were leaving. Where were they going?

The last cart passed him with a young boy perched on top looking off into nothing. Just before they disappeared into the mist the boy turned back and smiled at him. Then they were gone. He was left alone wondering after them. He felt he should follow and help, but some strong force kept him behind.

Two more times the same scene of loaded carts and mules with baskets unfolded to his view. No one spoke and none seemed to see him as he watched them except for the little boy. All were lost to the mist.

The first of five chimes snapped him awake.

It was always a similar dream. For the last several months he had seen the faceless people leaving to parts unknown. Sometimes on horses, sometimes in wagons and other times pulling carts themselves or walking.

The boy who smiled at him was the only unvarying feature of his dream. There was something about that face he should know, but for the life of him he couldn't figure out what it was.

◆

At precisely 8:00am JJ entered under the lion sculpture perched above the front door. The already bustling city outside was in stark contrast to the solitude he found in the anteroom. His boots sounded loud on the wood floor, somehow making him feel out of place.

"'Ello?" he called, not too loudly. No answer.

He waited a few more minutes wondering not for the first time what on earth he was doing here. Steeling himself, he decided as long as he was here he might as well see if anyone was around who could tell him how he could meet with

Brigham Young. He moved around the desk and down the long hall with closed doors on each side spaced at regular intervals. Was this a home or an office? It was hard to tell, but he decided it must be a little of both.

Even with the thick rugs as a buffer between his boots and the floor they still sounded loud to him. He came to an open door and peered inside.

A man with a beard was sitting at the desk it held writing something.

Clearing his throat, JJ said "Er, pardon me sir, but ah wonder if'n ya might help me?"

Glancing up, he said "I'll certainly do my best, young man. What is it you're looking for?"

"Well, ya see ah'm here fer a meetin' with Mr. Young, but ah can't find nobody 'round who could point me in the right direction."

The man behind the desk stood and smiled. "I bet I can point you in the right direction. Do you have an appointment?"

"No sir, ah shore don'. It's jes that ah come a long way ta see him 'bout sumthin'. Ah come all the way from Ioway with muh fam'ly. Kin ah git an appointment, ya think?"

"Why don't you sit down, son, and let me know what you want to talk to him about and then we'll see about setting up an appointment for you."

They both sat. "Alright, ah thankee, sir. Ah'l jes come right ta the point. Ah left home ta come here ta call 'im ta account fer hisself fer the shameful way he's treatin' them wimmen he calls wives. It jes ain't right an' ah mean ta git some sorter explanation fer his behavior."

The sentiments, held in for so long, finally came tumbling out of him in a rush. He felt sure this man would be shocked and deny him any chance of seeing Young. He didn't mention he'd first been thinking of hanging him. It seemed almost silly now.

Instead of being shocked, the man smiled again. Then the smile turned into a chuckle and ended with a hearty laugh. JJ was a little taken aback at this.

"Ah'm dead serious, sir. Ah've come a long way ta see him."

"So you have, so you have. I'm not trying to make light of your request - it's just so refreshing to see someone who gets straight to the point with no idle chit-chat. I take it you're a man of action?"

"Ah try ta be. If sumthin' needs doin' ah'l be doin' it. An' this's been ranklin' on muh last nerve fer some time now. Ah suppose ah won't be surprised if'n ya don't gimme an appointment, but ah'l tell ya, one way or t'other ah'm a gonna see him ta give him a piece a muh mind, sir."

"By all means! I wouldn't have it any other way for worlds. You will get your appointment, young man. Now let's see here...," he said, looking at a fancy, home-made calendar with squares for each day of the month.

"I see he's got a free space to squeeze you in tomorrow at 10:00am. Do you think you can state your opinion to him in under 30 minutes? He's got another appointment after that."

"Yessir, ah don' see a reason ah can't get it done by then."

"Who shall I say will be calling?"

"Muh name is Jerome Jefferson Adams. Ya kin put down JJ, if'n it's easier fer ya."

"JJ Adams. Yes, that fits better. JJ Adams to speak with Brigham Young at 10:00am tomorrow about polygamy and the evils thereof."

"Well, uh, yes, ah guess that 'bout sums it up. Do ya think he'll see me after all? He might not wanna talk 'bout it when ya put it that way."

"Son, I can guarantee you he will not only see you but talk to you about your concerns. You said you had your family with you here?"

"Yessir, muh wife an' two boys. One's jes a toddler an' the other is commin' up on a year old now. We also picked up another boy 'bout ten or so 'long the trail an' sorter adopted him, ya might say."

"That was good of you, I'm sure. Please bring your family with you when you come for your appointment tomorrow. Mr. Young will want to meet them. He loves children."

JJ thought about having Mary there with him as he took Young to task. "Ah'm not so sure that's a good idear, mister. This here's 'tween me an' Mr. Young."

"Nonsense. I doubt he'll see you alone. As I say, he loves children and he's a very busy man. We'll see you all at ten tomorrow morning. Now good day to you."

Standing at the abrupt dismissal, JJ wondered again what he'd gotten himself into.

"Uh, yessir. 'Til tomorrow then." He walked out and back down the hall. His boots didn't seem to make quite as much noise. A woman was sitting behind the desk who watched him emerge from the hall with a look of mild surprise.

"Ma'am," JJ said with a nod, then stepped through the door and out into the busy street.

◆

Mary had not wanted to come. Nevertheless, there she was with the three boys, all dressed in their best clothes, right along with JJ.

"But why would he want ta meet with us? I'm not the one who complained!" she had said. She was a little mad at JJ. After all, it wasn't her fight.

"Oh, honey, it won't hurt nothin'. The man ah talked ta said Young jes likes chil'ren. He probly wants ta make shore a'hm a good fam'ly man is all."

"Don't ya honey me. I'm not happy 'bout this a-tall."

So there they sat, the full hour lacking a few minutes, in an outer office much more full than the day before.

JJ looked around at the other folks trying to guess what brought them here. Several well-to-do looking men of business mixed with a middle-aged mother and her two teen-age boys. One who looked to be a blacksmith talked in low tones to a man dressed in buck skins.

Another man sat by himself, back to the wall, eyes never still, mentally weighing and measuring each of the other people in the room. He was dressed roughly and had a bushy full beard. It took a second look to verify the man was

61

armed although it shouldn't have – a huge revolver was strapped to his belt. It appeared well-used and the well-used looking man looked very used to the gun.

The same woman sat behind the desk. As the clock finished ten chimes, she looked at JJ pleasantly and said "You and your family can go in now. It's the same office you were in yesterday."

JJ stood and motioned Mary and the boys ahead of him. They all walked down the hall. "Right up thar," JJ said, indicating the open door to the right.

"Come right in, all of you please and take chairs." It was the same man from the day before. "I'll be right with you. I'm sure you don't mind if we have my special assistant sit in with us?"

JJ looked back and found to his surprise the armed man from the waiting room had followed them in. He hadn't even heard him behind them. He took a chair in one of the back corners of the office near a hat rack, never saying a word, but eyes ever watchful. JJ wondered what kind of things he assisted with.

So this was Brigham Young! JJ didn't like the fact that he'd been taken in so easily. His temper began a slow heat below the surface. A scowl fixed itself on his face. Mary noticed it and a worried look crossed hers.

Young must have noticed too. He chuckled softly as he looked at JJ with twinkling eyes. "Don't be perturbed, young man. I like to play jokes every now and again. You wouldn't rob an old man of his merriment would you? Don't think I was toying with you, either. I take you and your stated purpose very seriously, indeed. But before we go on, please introduce me to your family." He stood and came around the desk.

JJ had visibly relaxed at Young's easy manner. He stood also and his family with him, John Q looking up into the Mormon leader's face. "This here is muh wife, Mary, she's holdin' onta li'l Will who's almost a year old now. That thar is John Quincy named fer his president-cousin."

Young had been shaking hands at each introduction, but as he got to Edge his face took on an intense look. Tension rose noticeably in the room. Young dropped to one knee to stare into the youngsters face. "It's you. I know you. I've seen you before." Edge stared right back at him.

JJ was confused. "This's the boy we took on over ta Fort Kearny. We don' know his name on accounta he never talks. We been callin' 'im James fer now. Ya know 'im or his kinfolk?"

Young remained quiet for some time. The man in the corner stirred.

"No. I don't know him. I've never seen him before in the flesh. I have no idea who his parents are, either. You say he joined you at Fort Kearny?"

"Uh, it was a li'l before that. We come on 'im an' his pa jes a bit 'fore we got ta Kearny. At the fort the Major asked if we could take 'im 'long with us an' so here he be."

Young grasped his desk, stood and walked slowly around to sit down, obviously still deep in thought. JJ and Mary looked at each other and

64

slowly sat down as well. Uncomfortable minutes stretched before Young spoke again, almost to himself.

"This is most unexpected. The Lord does indeed work in strange ways His purposes to reveal. I have seen this young man many times before. He has been in a specific dream of mine. I've not known what it meant. I still don't, though I feel hopeful it will soon become more clear."

He looked up at their wondering faces. The man in the corner wore a knowing expression. "I'm sorry. I didn't mean to startle you. We can talk more of that later. For now, let's stick to what you came here for. As I remember you have traveled all the way from Iowa to give me a piece of your mind?" He smiled.

Mary shook her head slightly as JJ explained. "Well sir, it's really jes me. Ah felt like ah needed ta go ta Californy. Ah also wanted ta ask ya 'bout it. Them wives a-yers. It jes don' seem right no way ah kin put muh mind ta it."

"Have you read the Bible, specifically the Old Testament?" Young asked.

"Ah have. Ev'ry word in it."

"Very good. Then you know that many in those times had multiple wives."

"Yessir an' sumthin' called concubines too. Ah figured them's bein' jes 'bout like whores, not bein' married an' all."

Young chuckled again. "I've wondered about that myself. I've put it down to the culture and times they lived in according to the light and knowledge they possessed. Those concubines frequently became wives, though.

"However, that's not what I wanted to talk about. You see, we believe the Lord's church has been restored with His original Gospel. Another thing we believe is in continuing revelation. The Lord anoints who He will to lead His church and those have the spirit of revelation and prophecy. One such was Joseph Smith, who, one day, was reading in the Old Testament just like you have. He also wondered how those pious men could have had wives and concubines. He got an answer that he probably wasn't prepared for. The Lord commanded him to renew the practice."

JJ and Mary both looked skeptical – Young noticed, of course.

"I don't expect you to swallow that right off the bat. I'm simply explaining what we believe has been revealed. If we fail to follow His commandments, all of His commandments, we would find ourselves under condemnation as a people. We don't feel we can pick and choose what we will obey."

He sighed and went on. "However, most in the church don't choose to follow this commandment. Even some of those closest to me struggle with it. At any rate, that's what we believe and no force on earth will make us give up doing what we believe God has asked us to do. I don't relish it, but it's something I have learned to live with and see the wisdom of."

"But ah've heard tell a ver' young wimmen bein' taken as second or third wives ta some ver' ol' men. Now, that thar jes don' seem right," JJ said.

The man in the corner stifled a laugh. Young looked at him sternly.

"There may have been those who have abused the spirit of the law. We are not prefect beings, Mr. Adams. We try our best and every day we fall short – all of us. Hence the need for sincere prayer and repentance.

"However, I think we may be putting the cart before the horse. Since you have read the Bible, there's another book I'd like you to read, as well. It deals with the early history of the first people in this land. When you've read it I think we should meet again and finish discussing your concerns. Does that suit you?" He glanced at the clock which looked close to declaring the half hour.

"That'd be fine, sir, but ah have ta say money of any kind is scarce an' ah'm not shore spendin' it on a book is the best idear right now."

"This is to be a present from me to you and your family. It won't cost anything but your time to read it. Now, I hate to hustle you along but our time today has been spent. I hope that you feel it has been worth it. Feel free to call upon me when you like. You can make an appointment with Sister Jensen, who you've met this morning at the desk. Please don't leave the office until she has given you your book."

He rose and came around the desk to extend his hand. "Thank all of you for coming. Mrs. Adams it has been a pleasure." He looked again at Edge for a moment longer. "And you, young man, have some part to play in this that will yet be revealed." He smiled again as Edge stared up at him with big eyes.

"Porter, would you please show the Adams family out and then come back in here a moment?"

The bearded man merely nodded and escorted the family back to the front office.

"Dorothy, President Young wants you to give Mr. Adams here a copy of the Book of Mormon." He disappeared back down the hallway.

"Why, certainly. Here you are, Mr. Adams. Did President Young specify a time for you to return?"

"No ma'am, he din't. He jes said ta read the book an' come back when ah had."

"That's fine. When you'd like to schedule another appointment simply let me know. Good day to you all, then," she said with another smile at the boys.

Out on the porch JJ put his hat on and exchanged a dubious look with Mary. "Well, ah guess that's that. Now we kin git on our way ta Californy."

"You're not goin' ta read the book an' go back?"

"Hell no. Ah did what ah come fer. That ol' man seems sincere in his beliefs an' ah ain't gonna call 'im on em, but that don' mean ah'm a-gonna do what he says, neither.

"An' didya catch the name he called that other man? Porter. Ah'm guessin' that was none other than Porter Rockwell. His *special* assistant, he says. Ah'd have a hard time makin' any kinda trouble with him 'round. Not that ah wanna – ah changed muh mind after the way he 'splained hisself. But what was all that truck 'bout James?"

They both looked at Edge.

70

"I don' know. I surely don' know," Mary said thoughtfully.

◆

But later that afternoon, after his preparations for leaving the following morning had been completed, JJ belied his earlier words.

The boys were playing noisily around their wagon. Edge had come out of his shell just enough to have taken John Q and Will under his protective wing. Memories of his older brothers, especially Cass, naturally slid him into the older brother role. He still hadn't spoken, but his smiles and play with the younger boys made Mary's heart swell within her. She had hopes.

JJ would start the campfire for his wife's supper preparations in an hour or so, but in the meantime he found himself with some rare moments of inactivity. As was his habit when such times came, he opened the well-worn family Bible they had received as a wedding present

71

from Mary's folks. In it were listed their important dates – marriage, births and, unfortunately, the untimely deaths of his two daughters.

Books of any sort were rare for them. Not only were they expensive luxuries, but the weight of well-bound books added up. Libraries of more than ten books were unheard of being transported along the Oregon Trail by anyone other than well-to-do folks, teachers or fools.

The trails west were littered with the detritus of those unwise enough to pack too much furniture or too many clothes or books. A fully stocked library of classics could be picked up for free if someone was of such a mind. They had even seen an abandoned piano in Nebraska.

JJ closed the Bible and looked at the book Young's secretary had given him. It was handsomely bound, but not too heavy. He wondered who this Mormon fellow was. He'd never heard of any Indian named Mormon, but Young had said it was a history of early settlers in this country. He opened it and began reading.

◆

The time had passed for starting the fire, but a different sort of fire had been kindled as he read. The thirst for more knowledge burned in him.

Mary left him alone as she went about fixing their supper. It wasn't the first time JJ had gotten lost reading. Mostly it was the Bible, but she'd seen him lose track of time reading his Blackstone too.

During supper things were quiet. Mary was lost in her own thoughts of getting back on the trail the next morning and all that would entail. JJ was thinking about the book he had been reading and began to wonder if another visit to Young might be in order after all.

"You've been so quiet. Would ya like ta share your thoughts?" Mary asked after preparations for the night had been finished. The boys were snug in their blankets. Edge always threw his off anyway. She'd never seen someone who tossed and turned as much as he did. She noticed a gangly leg sticking out from under the blanket even now. Tucking that boy in did no good at all.

She'd also been noticing the tell-tale signs of change in herself – she knew she was pregnant again. The thought frightened her, with all the travel they still had ahead of them. At least the snow would be gone from the Sierra Nevada's in all except the highest peaks and passes.

The moment hadn't yet been right for her to broach the subject with her husband. She didn't want him worrying needlessly. She'd carry that load herself a little longer.

"Ah've been thinkin' ah might need ta go back an' talk ta that ol' man once more. Thar's things in this book that need some 'splainin'."

"Oh, no, JJ! It ain't more 'bout the wives, is it? I think that's jes a waste a time." She didn't want to think about having the baby on the trail – she was hoping to be in California by time her daughter was ready to be born.

Mary wondered when had she first thought of the baby as a she? Somehow the knowledge that another little girl was on the way seemed sure to her. She chilled a little thinking of her other two daughters left behind in Iowa.

JJ mistook her reaction. "Naw, it's other things than that. I jes need ta ask 'im a few questions. Won't take no time at all. Probly go tomorra mornin' first thing so's we kin git on the trail."

That would be alright then, Mary thought. As long as they didn't delay too long. A warm feeling came over her. She somehow felt assured this girl would be different and that everything would work out fine. Mary fell asleep with a calm, at peace feeling and a smile on her face.

◆

Brigham Young walked into his office and was startled to find JJ Adams waiting for him. Having just washed up after a lone breakfast, he wondered how JJ had gotten in. It was Saturday and no one was supposed to be in here until his usual 10:00 meeting with several church leaders.

"You're up early, young man! I didn't expect to see anyone for a few hours yet. You've a different look on your face than yesterday. What is it this time?" Young was a little put out at being taken by surprise this way.

"Well, sir, ah've come 'bout this here book ya gave me."

"Surely you haven't read the whole thing already!"

"Naw, but ah got quite a ways into it. Ah wanna know whar it come from, fer one thang, an' who wrote it fer 'nuther."

Young sat down and looked at JJ over his glasses. "There are several authors. Different prophets at different times kept the records of their people and it was passed down as each took their turn writing and taking care of the record.

"As for where it came from, that is a long story best saved for a time when we're not so hurried."

"We'll be on our way ta Californy this mornin'. Thar's another thing ah was meanin' ta ask ya 'bout. Yastidy ya looked our boy James over quite a bit. The missus an' ah would like ta hear

76

what it is ya recognize 'bout him. If'n ya know his kinfolk it'd be best ta let 'em in on whar-bouts he is."

Young looked at him evenly. "Do you believe in presentiments?"

"Ah wouldn't know one from 'nuther. What form do they take?"

"Dreams. Fore-tellings. Visions of things to come."

JJ looked skeptical. "Ah guess ah probly don' much. Now ya take Mary, muh wife, she thought mebbe ah'd been itchin' ta git goin' early jes so's we could be in the right place ta pick up James when we did. Mebbe jes a few hours made the diff'rence 'tween dead or alive with 'im. Ah'd been havin' feelin's like ah needed ta git out west fer some reason. That what yer talkin' 'bout?"

"That's part of it. The Lord's spirit works on people in different ways.

"But what I'm referring to is a dream I keep having. It's a lot of people moving to somewhere. It seems I am the one sending them but I don't know who they are or where they're going.

There's only one person I can remember – that boy you had with you. He's sitting on top of a loaded wagon and smiles at me just before they disappear. Just thinking about seeing that same face yesterday morning with you gives me goose-bumps. Why do you think that boy would be in my dreams?"

Feeling like every hair on the back of his neck was standing up, JJ studied the Mormon leader's face for any sign of deception. He found none. "Seems like mebbe yer gonna send 'im off somewhar's. But that don't make sense nohow. James'll be stayin' with us 'til we find any kinfolk a his'n."

Young looked thoughtful at that idea. For several minutes he seemed lost to someplace other than his office. The ticking of the clock was over-loud to JJ as the time stretched. Young finally spoke with a voice subtlety different.

"Do you know where the United States Army has the single largest body of troops stationed anywhere right now?"

"Nary an idear. Ah'd 'spect somewhar 'round Washington or back east on accounta that whole slave question." JJ wondered what that had to do with James.

"You'd think so. Instead, it's right down the way near Fairfield, not but a few miles from where we sit. The President himself sent them here to put down a supposed rebellion."

JJ shifted in his seat uncomfortably remembering his own reason for coming. "Well, ya gotta know how much folks're against that whole idear 'bout polygamy an' such."

Young smiled and seemed to look right into him. "Yes, I've been made aware of those types of feelings. Anyhow, when the army leaders found no rebellion and nothing but a peaceable people only trying to build up a civilization and city to our God as we saw fit, they decided to camp their army down the road. You said something about going to California to raise beef for miners?"

"Yessir, that's the plan."

"Fairfield is a stage stop as well as a station for the new Pony Express on the trail to where you're headed. I wonder if you might consider staying in that area to raise your cattle there for a time.

"I know the army has bought up almost everything around. Even though the cash money helps, we find ourselves needing more beef and horses and mules and just about everything the army has used up.

"They get resupply from Fort Leavenworth, but it's a massive effort keeping that many men in supplies.

"You'd have a guaranteed market for everything you could possibly raise, between them and us here in Salt Lake City. I have some land near there that I could lease to you at a very low rate, if you're interested."

Having wondered several times how he was going to get the land he needed to raise his beef herd, JJ sat a little straighter in his chair considering the possibility.

"How much do ya think ah'd need ta start out an' what kinda rate is a low rate?"

"You'd be helping the folks around here a lot, so how does a rate of a penny per acre, per year, sound to you? I can lease you almost 500 acres in the valley leading to Flat Top Mountain and you could graze your cattle and horses on many more thousands of acres in the surrounding mountains for nothing. That works out to about $5.00 per year."

JJ had never dreamed of so much land. His mind spun at the sudden opportunity.

Young slapped his desk and went on: "I have a good feeling about you, Mr. Adams. I think I can see a way to kill several birds with one stone. I'll be perfectly frank with you - it also wouldn't do any harm to have someone such as you as another set of eyes on those soldiers. They are subject to doing whatever their leaders allow them to. So far they've stayed pretty much away from the city, but that could change at any moment."

"Now jes hold yer horses. Ah'll not be no stool-pigeon fer any man. Ah'm not so sure which side ah come down on yet. Like as not ah could be heppin' them army boys if it came ta it."

81

Young laughed. "I didn't mean it that way. You'd be no spy. But we would need to keep the lease deal strictly between us – if the army found out, you could have some rough going of it. They've no love for me.

"I'm simply thinking of my people here and the relative lack of certain provisions now that the Amy has been here a few years. They do get resupply from Leavenworth but that is over 1,100 sometimes hostile miles away. The market should be very good for an enterprising young man. Is that you or have I missed my judgment?"

"Ever since we left Ioway we been headin' fer Californy. Ah'll need ta think this here over an' talk with the missus too."

"By all means. I'd not thought of any of this until just this morning here talking with you. It feels right, but absolutely you need to think on it. Study it out. Go visit the land and see if you think it will work for you.

"When you've made up your mind come back or send word. We can get the details worked out

82

at that point so everything is legal." Hastily he drew a crude map and gave it to Adams.

JJ stood, took the map and extended his hand. "That listens good, mister Young. Ah thankee fer the kind consideration an' ah'll be lettin' ya know soon, one way or t'other."

"Don't forget to keep reading your book!" Young said as JJ turned to leave.

JJ smiled and nodded.

Camp Floyd / Fairfield

The Adams' first sight of the nearly 400 buildings the U.S. Army had erected made them all stare. It was said over 7000 people lived at Camp Floyd, named for the current Secretary of War, which was almost half of what lived in Salt Lake City itself.

A notorious southern sympathizer, it was also rumored that John B. Floyd was doing his best to drain the treasury ahead of a likely war with the south, what with how much it cost to keep the massive troop concentration supplied. Many thought it was also a neat way of tying up army resources far from any conceivable places of battle.

JJ turned the team towards the northwest and into the canyon Young had showed him on the map. The ground in many places was very poor. In others, natural grasses as well as other types of low growing, hardy, desert plants dotted the landscape.

It appeared the grazing would work as long as he was able to keep the cattle near enough to the natural water sources so they didn't have to walk the meat off getting from graze to drink.

The mountains were tip-tilt to the rest of the valley - it didn't look like they'd be much use beyond looking at. Not many head of cattle did JJ think they'd be able to support.

When he had brought up the subject of ranching in the mountains to the southwest of Salt Lake City, instead of California as had been their plan, he had been surprised at how quickly Mary had agreed they should look into it.

He didn't have to wonder very long as to the reason – he was a happy man when Mary announced she was going to have a little girl. That they wouldn't be on the trail for the birth was an obvious relief for his wife. He felt a little ashamed he hadn't noticed her showing already. Now that he knew, he felt inattentive for missing it before.

He'd have his hands full building a small mud house in time for them to live in, not to mention the corrals and pens and fences required for the cattle and horses he planned on. All needed to be completed before the snow began to fly – it was sooner here than Sidney, he had heard. He had at most maybe three months to do it all in, which was also around the time Mary was due. It was a tall order.

He had been supplied with all he could think of they might need before winter set in. Ten horses and thirty or so head of cattle were to follow, driven in by a few discreet men hand-picked by Porter Rockwell, along with another wagon-load of provisions.

Everything was paid for by JJ's "silent" partner. He had found out to his chagrin Young wasn't silent about almost anything and was very interested and voluble about exactly how he thought JJ ought best to proceed.

Since Young was bankrolling the whole thing, JJ just listened and nodded. Besides, Young did have some good ideas at that - it was obvious he had been thinking of this project for some time.

◆

The autumn of 1860 sprouted wings and flew away leaving the weight of yet another hard winter pressing down the Adams clan on their fledgling ranch. Edge turned out to be a big help even though he still never said anything.

Store-bought feed was brought from Salt Lake by the brimming wagon full. Horses and cattle stayed in their respective pens and were hand-fed through that first winter.

A well had been dug on the place they decided to stay and JJ kept himself busy freeing their water supply of ice.

In between times he made improvements to their small home and the stock corrals and pens. The animals never strayed since they didn't have to find their own feed. JJ's husbandry improved as he became more in tune with them through close practice.

It was a hard but enjoyable life. The whole family pitched in, even Mary, though she frequently had her hands full with little Martha, who had arrived without incident in November.

Edge became the perfect older brother as he doted on all three of the children, but especially Martha. Mary sometimes wondered what they'd do if relatives of his showed up to claim him. They had written to Major Spader at Fort Kearny to let him know where they were, but had received no reply.

They had also written to their parents back in Iowa to let them know they were doing well. The return letter brought news - his younger brother,

Byron, had moved onto JJ's old farm and was making a go of being a farmer, his father reported. William also inquired as to whether he and Temperance should come out themselves.

JJ could think of nothing better and encouraged them to do so. However, in the time it took for his return letter to travel to Sidney, momentous events intruded, and it was never to be.

A new republican president had been elected, Abraham Lincoln, who ran opposed to the expansion of slavery into the new western territories.

Before he could be inaugurated, seven southern states seceded from the union to form the Confederacy.

On the 12th of April, 1861, the first shots were fired at Fort Sumter in South Carolina, which would come to multiply exponentially and eventually claim the lives of more than 600,000 soldiers.

As it did on countless others, the ensuing war had a profound effect on the JJ Adams family, with many consequences, both unimagined and unimaginable, still far in the future.

The most immediate and evident of these was the decampment of Camp Floyd (now renamed Fort Crittenden) when the army was recalled to much more important duties than watching Mormons.

By late August of 1861 only a handful of families remained in the Fairfield area, one of which was the stalwart Adams bunch, attempting to raise beef for the suddenly deserted market.

Now we must leave JJ, Mary and the children to their own devices for a few decades and turn our attention eastward.

◆

Part II

Tennessee – Texas

Pittsburg Landing, Tennessee – April 6, 1862

Able Bellows peeked over the small rise toward where the Union Army reportedly lay concealed in the lands just west of the Tennessee river.

Was it possible the North had six divisions stationed in that area? Their spies said so, but that would amount to more than 40,000 men. Able couldn't see room for so many.

The sun was beginning to lighten the eastern sky. Soon, they'd be given their final instructions for the surprise attack against Grant's forces.

They'd been moving all night under orders from General Johnston – a little over 40,000 men of their own spoiling for a fight with the despised Yankees.

91

After losing Fort Donelson and Fort Henry in February, control of the Tennessee and Cumberland rivers had fallen to the Union.

But Able knew General Johnston thought he could wipe out a big part of the Union Army with one surprise counterstroke. His plan was to push them into the swamps to the west and destroy them before General Buell could arrive with the Army of the Ohio in relief.

Able had lost track of his brother Broc shortly after arriving to join the Confederacy in Tennessee.

When war had broken out a year earlier, both brothers had talked about what they should do. Sentiments around St. Joseph were mixed - Missouri was a slave state but had remained in the Union.

The two elder brothers leaned toward sympathy for personal liberty and individual property rights. It appeared to them the federal government was running roughshod over anything that got in its way.

They agreed it should be up to the citizens of the territories to vote what they thought best for their own area. Lincoln resolved against leaving it to the people to decide about slavery in a potential state. In fact, he'd won the presidency with that position.

With their father a year gone, surprisingly the remaining four Bellows brothers had done well. Able and Broc were the natural leaders, but Cass and Dirk pitched in as well. They had all decided they would make what they could of the farm until their father returned and all worked toward that goal.

The ground finally thawed and they were able to plant the seed carefully saved from the previous year's harvest. Nature lent a hand, as if knowing she'd been fickle by shortening the growing season with the hard winter – rains came at the proper time mixed with enough sunny days to ensure bounteous harvests throughout the region.

The boys worked at fixing up the house and barn and adding to them. Unstated was the desire to please a long-gone father they had no way of knowing was dead. Each hoped to see him and their little brother Edge roll back into the yard. As time passed so did their hopes dwindle. But still they toiled together to improve the farm and their efforts were rewarded.

Even though they worked as hard as their older two brothers, neither Cass nor Dirk liked farming. They talked to each other about drifting southwards toward Texas, where they had heard the cattle industry was booming and wide open.

While duty called Able and Broc, the two younger boys had no strong feelings either way. They were more opportunistic and took after their father in that respect.

As the fruits of their labors multiplied, they found themselves in a position to buy things they never thought possible. Soon the homestead had horses in the corrals, more mules for plowing, two milk cows and more chickens than they'd ever had when their father had been there. They had also bought a second-hand wagon to replace the old and broken one.

The place actually looked good.

Then the South tried to break the nation. No one was really taken off-guard when it happened. In fact, Able was surprised it took so long to start.

Emotions ran high both north and south of the Mason-Dixon line. Both sides felt a righteous indignation towards the other – while Dixie might not completely support the institution of slavery, almost everyone in the South agreed it should be up the individual states and territories to decide for themselves. They thought the Constitution protected them against the federal government taking their "property".

Northerners, on the other hand, felt the only way to get rid of slavery as a national stain was to legislate at the national level.

First, in 1852, Harriet Beecher Stowe had horrified them with *Uncle Tom's Cabin.* Then the Supreme Court followed five years later with the *Dred Scott* decision, which overturned the Missouri Compromise banning slavery above the

36-30 parallel and basically said black Americans had no rights whatsoever.

What was next, the North wondered? Slavery was now technically legal throughout the United States.

Such an evil thing had to be stamped out whether southerners liked it or not. Lincoln favored letting it naturally die as new territories came into the Union as "free" states, but that wasn't fast enough for northern abolitionists.

Neither Able nor Broc cared even a bit for the idea of slavery, but they didn't like being told what to do, either.

General Albert Sidney Johnston was a popular figure in the south and a capable commander who had control of the entire southern army from the Cumberland Gap all the way to Arkansas. The older two boys figured it was past time to join up.

"I still don' think ya should go. That'll be two less folks ta lend a hand." Cass Bellows was 16 now. He figured himself a man and did a man's work just as the other boys did. His little brother

Dirk didn't talk a lot, but never missed a thing. As usual, he sat and watched silently.

"Lookie here, you two. We been over this a thousand times or more. It's probly not gonna take long to throw them Yankees back where they belong, but it's gotta be done by someone. You know what pa would want us to do," replied Broc.

Able nodded. "An' we're of the age where we can't ignore it. Y'all are a little too young or we'd all be goin', more'n likely."

"Not me. We're westerners an' it ain't our fight. I say let 'em beat up on each other, but leave us outa it."

"Cass, you know Missouri oughta be part of the Confederate States – hell, it's a slave state already! We gotta fight fer our rights! Jes like we had to in the revolutionary war," said Broc.

"Missouri might be a slave state, but we ain't never had us no slaves an' never will. All I know is pa up an' left an' we ain't never heard a thing. Now you two are leavin'? Dirk an' me are gonna be all that's left a the Bellows fam'ly."

97

"Broc an' me ain't pa," Able said. "We'll be back afore ya know it."

It went on. Dirk listened to them all with expressionless eyes. He wouldn't say it, but he really didn't care one way or the other.

◆

That had been eight months ago. To Able it seemed like eight years.

He and Broc had found the western part of the Confederate Army camped at the Mississippi in Arkansas, but were sent east to join up with General Tilghman at Fort Henry. Broc had been sent further on down the swampy road to Fort Donelson.

For both of them the next few months held nothing but sheer boredom. They drilled and practiced shooting their ancient flintlock rifles. They learned how to load, aim and fire the 32-pounder cannons. Some of the troops said their rifles were left over from the War of 1812, but Able couldn't believe they were that old.

Then on February 6th, Union General Ulysses S. Grant attacked Fort Henry utilizing seven gunboats under the command of United States Navy officer Andrew Foote.

With the river at flood stage and the fort's powder magazine under water, Tilghman realized the position was untenable.

On the 5th, anticipating Union infantry at the fort at any time, he had ordered Colonel Heiman to take most of the troops the 12 miles to Fort Donelson. By then Able was a sergeant of the infantry and marched in the almost 4,000 strong body of southerners.

Left with less than 100 infantry and nine guns still above water, Tilghman had just one objective: hold for at least an hour to give the main body of his men more time to escape. This he did, striking the flag and running up a white sheet in its place 75 minutes after the battle started.

Just hours after Fort Henry fell the Tennessee river covered it completely.

◆

Broc Bellows hunkered down beneath the huge sycamore tree and waited for the rain to ebb. He was part of a reconnaissance patrol sent out from Colonel Trabue's brigade to see where Union General Grant's forces lie and in what strength. The first brigade was under the command of General Breckinridge whose Corps was supposed to be held in reserve during the anticipated battle.

If the rain didn't let up it would make it difficult to attack this morning as had been the plan.

So far Broc had seen no fighting since his platoon of westerners had been transferred away from Fort Donelson a week before it fell. Trabue needed scouts who could move without being detected and felt some of the Missouri boys might be just the thing.

Broc was happy to get away from the boredom of fort-sitting. It wasn't what he signed up for. They drilled incessantly, marching to and fro, and when they weren't drilling all he had to do was watch the Cumberland river go by. He wanted action. Since arriving he had become even more convinced he was on the right side. The Yankees needed to mind their own business.

It was almost full light now. The rain had slowed enough so that Sergeant Ruebush (the boys all called him Sarg Rubbish) decided to move forward. The whispered orders came and Broc stood for his normal duty at point. He was proud to have been considered for such an important job. If his pa could only see him now!

The patrol was in the middle of an open space when several shots rang out to his right. Instinctively everyone dropped.

"Get up ya ijuts! They ain't firin' at us!" Ruebush growled at them. "Bellows, git goin' up an' ta the left 'bout a hunnerd yards ta them trees yonder. Move it!"

They moved it.

Broc hoped his powder had stayed dry with all the rain. He could now see clouds of smoke less than half a mile away. He felt exposed even running at a half-crouch. His gear rattled. It seemed they all made way too much noise even with everything else as loud as it suddenly was and the wet grass.

They finally made it to the stand of trees only to discover they were the second group to get there. The first was dressed in blue – ironically, it was part of the 25th Missouri infantry.

◆

Able hadn't heard the command to open fire. He didn't even see anyone to shoot at. But all of sudden everyone was shooting at something and reloading.

The men were spread out in a line that stretched for one hundred feet on either side of Able. Slowly they advanced a step, jump and squat at a time. Explosions shook the ground under his boots. The pop of rifles was answered by more.

They pushed back at the Yankees little by little. Hour after hour the southern wave urged forward uncertainly. Men fell all around him only to be replaced by soldiers he didn't know. Able so far had been lucky by escaping any harm himself, but it was little solace for the number of his friends he had seen lost that morning.

Once, while trotting forward, he tripped on a log that wasn't a log - it was a dead Union soldier. Noticing the rifle the Yankee had used was far better than his musket he switched. He found the powder charges and caps in a possibles bag, slung it around his neck and continued on.

The firing on both sides had become sporadic. Confused Confederate soldiers were milling in a group of at least 400 when Able joined them. Several officers on horses rode in.

"Boys, my name is Ruggles, and I know most of you have been separated from your units. It's been a bloody fight, but we've got 'em on the run!" A hearty cheer went up from the tired men.

"We've charged at least a dozen times and pushed back both of their flanks. I've ordered up some heavy cannon from the rear. We'll wipe out the rest of this damned hornet's nest and push them yanks on into the river. Y'all rest a while at that church over yonder a piece, but stay hitched. We're gonna finish this today come hell or high water - probably both!"

He didn't wait to hear their additional cheer, but galloped away to the south towards another group of dingy, grey-coated soldiers while they stared after him.

The weary men gathered their guns and equipment and trudged toward the lonely little meetinghouse with a Hebrew name that meant "the one to whom it belongs".

They had no way of knowing Shiloh Church would become famous and symbolize the beginning of the end for the south.

◆

That's a funny color for the sky, Broc thought. *Why would it be red? An' why am I looking at the sky, anyhow?*

Suddenly Bub Johnson's face blocked his view. His lips were moving and he looked concerned, but Broc couldn't make out the words. Slowly sound returned to the world.

"I said - are ya alright, Corporal?" Bub asked again.

Broc realized he was lying on his back, looking up at his friend. He couldn't feel a thing. He thought *Yes, I'm fine. Why wouldn't I be?* But his mouth wouldn't speak the words out loud for some reason.

He remembered Bub was from some tiny town in South Carolina. His name was Bubba but everyone called him Bub. *I never found out what his real name was. Maybe it's Bubba.*

105

"Ya got shot. We gave em what-fer, but I can't see nobody else. Ya hang on - I'm gonna go find some he'p."

I got shot? Broc tried to move. Nothing happened. He couldn't see Bub anymore and he couldn't turn his head.

Suddenly he felt cold all over. And thirsty. He was so thirsty. He couldn't remember what water tasted like. *Bub, please bring me some water.*

The sky is darker than it should be for this time of morning. Why is it so dark?

He thought of his brothers back in Missouri. He wished he was there too. *Sorry, boys. I don't think I'm a-gonna make it.* A tear escaped the corner of one eye.

Broc shivered a final time and his whole body relaxed. *So cold out here...*

Bub shouted down at Corporal Bellows. Sergeant Ruebush laid his hand on Bub's shoulder.

"It's no use - he's dead, son. Nothin' we kin do now. He's gone ta God. We gotta git movin' or we'll be joinin' 'im at them pearly gates." He

106

settled his coat over Bellows face and moved cautiously away.

Bub stood and then stooped to pick up his rifle. He'd known Broc only a short time, but he had been a good sort of man. Bub had trouble understanding the reason good men died that quickly.

He wasn't the first and wouldn't be the last to ask the same question that bloody day. Or other days in other places and times immemorial.

He gave Broc a final salute and followed his sergeant.

◆

The men moved forward with care. Even though the Union soldiers had their rifles raised above their heads, the fighting had been so intense Able and his men could be excused for being suspicious.

The half-hundred cannons and an eternity of shelling had finally taken it's toll – the remaining troops under the command of Union General Prentiss surrendered.

But not without a terrible price for the south. General Johnston was dead – bled to death of a gun shot wound to his leg. Refusing his own surgeon's attentions in favor of his wounded and dying men, he had inadvertently sacrificed his own life.

With his death, General Beauregard, a much less aggressive leader, took command and the southern advantage was not pressed until it was too late. It was to be a turning point in the war.

Prentiss had also bought precious time with his holding the "Hornet's Nest" as it came to be known. That time allowed for the regrouping of the Union Army around Pittsburg Landing, now fortified on the left flank by the arrival across the river of a full brigade from Bull Nelson's division.

Able was haunted by the sounds that night; the groans and pleas of the dying filled his ears until their supplications faded mercifully away.

With complete carnage on both sides it was the bloodiest day in American history to that point. It would get worse the following day and for years to come, but Able would never know it.

Even though there was still more than a half-million soldiers yet to die on both sides before Appomattox Court House, Shiloh essentially finished the Confederacy.

The battle was especially hard on one family from Missouri as it would claim the life of a second Bellows brother the final day of fighting.

Belknap, Texas – June, 1866

The vast herd of longhorns stretched as far into the distance as Cass could see in the waning light.

He was on night-herd that evening having just relieved his little brother, Dirk. There were six other riders on duty that night.

The next day, all 17 punchers and the huge chuck wagon holding their provisions, driven by the cook, would start the more than 2,000 head on a drive to the northwest and the planned terminus of Fort Sumner in the New Mexico Territory.

The trail bosses were also the owners of the cattle - former Texas Ranger Charles Goodnight and Oliver Loving. Both of them tough as nails and as good or better cowboys than their hired hands, they figured on selling the beef to the military outposts along the way, as well as to Indian agents for the Navajo recently located on reservations around Fort Sumner.

It was a bold venture and chock-full of risks. But the potential rewards were enormous. The wild beasts were virtually free for the adventurous cattleman's gathering.

Navaho Indians were starving in New Mexico and each pair of horns represented gold on the hoof at almost a dime per pound. Legends were in the making.

◆

Never having heard from either of their older brothers during the war, Cass and Dirk decided to sell the farm soon after the surrender of Lee.

They'd worked as hard as they could making little improvements here and there and when the war ended the farm was in decent shape – worth enough to get them on the trail south to Texas.

"Rye Parks says he's gonna come by tomorrow with the rest a the payment on this place. I told him he could have it lock, stock an' barrel minus our horses an' truck, a-course," Cass said to Dirk as the two sat drinking coffee at the table in what served as their kitchen. He looked around the room.

"He an' the missus got a passel a tow-headed chil'ren. I wonder whar they're gonna put 'em?"

Dirk didn't look up. "Who cares? Long as he brings the rest a thet gold they kin toss 'em in the barn fer all I know about it. I'm ready ta git shut a this place."

"Ya know we gotta put some a thet money aside in case Broc or Able ever shows up. It's part theirs too."

111

"I don't see how. We're the ones been workin' it an' makin' it what it is. Wasn't fer us there wouldn't be no farm," Dirk said.

"More'n likely. But we still got it ta do." Cass was insistent.

"They probly got theirselves kil't anyway. Useless. They ain't never showin' up nowhere."

"Ya may be right. But I think we need ta take five double-eagles an' jes set 'em aside. Thet still leaves each a us with fifty dollars a piece, plus our horses an' gear. We'll leave a note with Parks 'bout whar we're goin' an' if they don't show in a year, we'll split the rest. Thet's fair, doncha think?"

Dirk considered his brother carefully. He didn't particularly like the idea, but he respected Cass.

"No, I don' think it's fair, but I'm not gonna buck ya if it'll shut ya up about it." He grinned.

Cass laughed. "Damn, I think I'd rather take on a badger with a short stick than tangle with ya."

Dirk looked at him over the rim of his cup. He knew Cass wasn't afraid of him. But he might ought to be.

◆

All kinds of cattle, but mostly the rangy longhorns, had been running wild and free in Texas all during the Civil War. When it ended, enterprising men had gotten together to round them up into large herds.

Those cattle could take care of themselves. They'd stood for years against coyotes and wolves and bears. A body just about couldn't get them if they didn't want to get-got. They turned boys into hands and hands into top-hands. Those horns could catch a man's thigh or cripple a horse or worse. It was dangerous work.

Cass and Dirk had drifted into the Weatherford area west of Fort Worth at just the right time. They wanted to work cattle and there was nowhere on earth that presented such work

113

with more of a challenge. They hired on with the Goodnight and Loving outfit never realizing they'd be helping blaze a cattle trail destined to go down in history.

Elm Creek – 1876

"We'd like a job if'n yore hirin'," Cass told the older man.

J.R. Couts surveyed the two cowboys with scant interest. He'd seen a hundred more just like them in the last year. Hard-bitten, trail-weary and down on their luck.

Still, they rode good horse flesh and both had Winchesters in saddle boots. The silent one was wearing a new Colt.

"Y'all know cattle?" Couts spat tobacco juice on a large black ant. It swam for a while and regained its footing just in time to be drowned again.

"Yessir, we shore do. Drifted down from Missouri in '66. Drove with Mr. Goodnight on his first ta New Mexico an' ag'in the next year when injuns scattered the herd. We took part of thet bunch on ta Denver while he went back ta tend ta Mr. Loving.

"Kept on with Goodnight an' later with Mr. Chisum when they hooked up ta send cattle north into Colorado reg'lar-like.

"We figured ta come back ta whar we started an' heard ya might be lookin' fer hands out here. Hoped ta find another job wrastlin' the critters we know."

Couts considered while he watched the ant struggle. "Ya rode fer Chisum?"

"Yessir, the both a us on drives. We jes come back from Wyomin'."

"No cattle work in Wyomin', huh?"

Cass shifted his feet. "Well, sir, about thet thar — we jes figured ta come on down here whar it's a might warmer, ya could say."

Couts glanced at Dirk whose stony face gave away nothing.

115

"Fer me, I'm guessin' the pair a ya wore out a welcome in Wyomin' an' it wasn't the weather what done it."

The older man had come pretty close to the truth when Cass told him who they had ridden for.

The Bellows brothers were known for two things – they were both excellent cowboys and not shy about using their guns. Especially the younger one, Dirk.

"Heard tell of a coupla boys 'bout yore age. Name a 'Bellows', if I recall correctly an' I reckon I do. They seem ta be handy with a gun or a cow-critter even up. Y'all ever heard a anyone like thet up in Wyomin'?"

"We be them Bellows," Dirk spoke for the first time. He stared at Couts who looked right back evenly. There was no scare in the man.

Cass broke in. "Thar's a lot a stories folks tell, but it don't make...."

Couts held up his hand to stop the explanation. "Out here, you young fellows have ta do ta git along. I'll not judge a man by campfire gossip.

116

How-some-ever, I *will* judge 'im by what he *says* he kin do an' what he *really* kin do. If y'all rode with Goodnight an' Chisum, I kin use ya on the Hashknife. It's thet simple. I pay thirty a month an' two-bits each found. When I see fer myself what yore about you'll git $45 a month top-hand wages. How's thet sound?"

Cass looked at Dirk who nodded almost imperceptibly.

"Yessir, thet goes."

"Good. Go report ta Shorty. He's the tall redhead. Tell 'im I said ta start ya breakin' the wild ones the mex's brung in t'other day. We'll see what kinda cowboys y'are right off.

"An' boys? No gun play 'round this here headquarters. Wouldn't want anyone gettin' shot accidental-like." He gave Dirk an appraising eye.

Dirk drew rein and laughed. "Nope. We shore wouldn't, Mr. Couts. I kin almost guarantee ya no one will git shot accidental by us."

◆

It took a week for the brothers to become $45 hands. The work was hard but of a kind they knew and were used to.

The Hashknife was boot-strapped in an unforgiving land by gathering wild and ornery longhorns with sometimes wilder and ornery-er men. The Bellows fit right in.

Their reputation was known and the other hands were aware, if not necessarily wary. Practically no one hired on at the Hashknife wasn't some kind of hard case. It's what the life and times demanded.

They were the breed of men available - softness was ruthlessly weeded out. The weak either died from any of the myriad dangers or they returned broken to the east.

Word was Dirk had killed several men and was supposed to be fast on the trigger.

Their horses had left Cheyenne just ahead of a riled populace and the Bellows decided to go along for the ride. The shooting had been fair, but the man had friends.

Cass had never killed anyone and didn't want to. But he had pulled Dirk out of more sticky situations than he cared to remember. He was known as a bad man with which to tangle by simple association with a true bad-man. The two were always together as a team, so it was assumed Cass was also *un hombre malo*.

Abilene – September, 1882

When J.R. Couts sold his Hashknife interests to the Continental Land and Cattle Company it brought the total number of cattle the new St. Louis-based company owned to more than 50,000 in Baylor county alone.

The ranch by then extended hundreds of miles westward to the Pecos river in the New Mexico Territory, but even with so vast a range, over-grazing was becoming a problem.

The Texas and Pacific Railway was busy building through the panhandle of West Texas. The new ranch owners realized they could ship their cattle by rail to the eastern markets and reduce the dangers and expense of trail drives to far-off rail heads, so they lobbied the T&P to route the line straight through their Hashknife ranch. The new town of Abilene sprung into existence as a result.

It was a rough and tumble town in the very beginning – practically owned by the ranch. Hashknife cowboys took many liberties without any resulting consequences. Bullets frequently declared the law. The tough and the quick men ruled the roost, Dirk Bellows foremost among them.

His bosses at the Continental gave him wide berth. Other hands, hard men in their own right, did the same. No one seemed to know what to do with him. Unlike Cass, who was well-liked and a genuine top cowman, Dirk inspired mostly fear in those around him. He had become lazy as a result and even Cass hesitated calling him on it.

Dirk had taken to hanging around the Lucky Jack Saloon in Abilene at the expense of the job he got paid top-hand wages for. As he'd always done, Cass picked up the slack for his little brother, but it was wearing thin on him.

They sat together in companionable silence at a table in the Jack.

"I been thinkin' a drifting west a ways," Cass offered. "Mebbe try ta find a place a muh own I kin homestead an' run a few cows over ta New Mexico."

Dirk studied his brother with a slight smile. "Ya lookin' ta git shet a me?"

"Naw, ya know ya'll always be muh partner. I was askin' if'n ya might wanna side me. I got enough money set aside ta buy me a little herd off them Continental boys. I figure ta drive 'em ta some little valley fur 'nuff west a the Pecos thet I don't see me no more Hashknife cows ever. Someplace we kin git water an' file papers. With ya along we could file on more'n 300 acres."

"Partners, huh? Waal, brother, it wouldn't be much of a partnership if I don't got no investment money."

121

"Ya could work off yore share. We could call it the CD. Mebbe even put the D on a rocker or make it lazy." Cass grinned.

"Ya got sumthin ta say jes go right ahead," Dirk said coldly.

"Aw now, Dirk, don't be thet way! I was jes funnin' ya's all. I'm serious 'bout movin' on, though. Ever since we rode with Chisum I been partial ta thet country."

"I know it. This 'round here ain't a patch on them mountains. Ya think thar might be a place left we could git without havin' ta jump it? Not thet I wouldn't mind it if the place was good enough," he teased his brother.

Cass didn't like that idea but kept quiet about it.

"It's a big country. Thar's gotta be some place left ain't got folks squatted on it yet."

"Ya let me think on it a-while, why doncha?" Dirk already knew he didn't want that kind of life but he wasn't going to tell Cass that yet.

"Alright. Ya jes lemme know when ya made up yore mind.

122

"Thar's one other thing - I hate ta even name it ta ya, but some a the boys been grumpin' ya don't pull yore weight 'round here. Now don't go flyin' off the handle. Yore a top-hand, but ya know ya been slackin' fer a while now."

Dirk had a sour expression on his face. "Them yella bellies had ta get ya ta haul their freight, eh? If'n they're so all-fired took about it, they kin jes run the specifics by me their-own-selves. I ain't heard no complainin' yet with my own ears."

"Like I said – I hate namin' it ta ya. Yore a great cowboy, but yore heart ain't been in it."

Dirk relented. "Yore right 'bout thet," he sighed. "My heart ain't in it no more, but I don't know nothin' else. I'm gettin' more surly by the day. I feel like a bear with a sore tooth."

Cass had never seen his brother look so forlorn. He suddenly felt ashamed of the part he'd taken in the discussions behind Dirk's back about what could be done. He changed tacks.

"Ya 'member when Able an' Broc left fer the war an' all we had ta do was work on thet bitty 'ol farm?"

123

Dirk nodded thoughtfully. "I do. They were a coupla fools."

"It was jes you an' me an' I think the both a us knew we weren't gonna see them boys ag'in. We was workin' fer ourselfs - ta git a stake so's we could come down here an' chous the cows aroun'.

"What say we do thet here on this job with the eye towards gettin' us our own place out in them mountains? I know the bosses a this spread would sell us critters fer less than we could git 'em somewhar else. Probly jes ta git shut a us."

Dirk chuckled. "Ya mean me." He leaned forward, thinking about it. "But ya might have sumthin thar. This job don't make me feel like I'm workin' towards anythin'. If'n we had our own place, I might could take a-holt ag'in. Ya really wanna give 'er a try?"

"Yup, I do. It's a little late ta start a drive this year, but come spring I say we give it a chance. Ya done thinkin' 'bout it a'ready? Ya in, little brother?"

Somehow Dirk knew this was as good an offer as he was likely to get from any direction.

"I'm done thinkin'. I'm in."

May, 1884

Six months turned into 18.

His attitude shifted by working for a goal, Dirk had become a different man. He was still no *hombre* take lightly, but now he was respected as a cowboy to ride the range or river with, as well.

The boss noticed and tried talking the brothers out of leaving for the high pastures of New Mexico.

But Dirk had by then also saved enough money that the two of them together could afford a small herd of 250 yearlings, a decent *remuda* and a chuck wagon to carry their provisions.

Bryant Mays, a solid block of muscle with a ready smile who stood just about as wide as he did tall, recently of Montana, decided to throw in with them. He would drive the wagon and cook - he had a well-deserved reputation for dutch-oven mastery.

125

Dirk had a new lease on life as they all discussed and made their preparations. Cass felt thankful for that short talk they'd had in Abilene - it had made all the difference.

They didn't know precisely where they'd end the drive, but the brothers were as versed as anyone about the cattle trails of the west - trails they had helped forge. They knew where they could find water. Where to stop for graze and shelter. Where many of the dangers lurked.

And yet, how carefully we prepare our puny construction plans only to have the Master Architect further reveal His mind for the building!

One of the three would never make it out of Texas after his horse fell with him.

Another would lose his scalp and life, in that order, to Apaches after a rolling battle in the New Mexico Territory.

The last, luckiest of that luckless trio, thoroughly disillusioned and discouraged, would escape the New Mexico natives with his life, but minus his most everything else, only to be recruited by the same brand he'd thought left for good in Texas.

The remaining Hashknife cattle, more than 30,000 strong, moved north and west from the Pecos to a vast new range, a million acres by 650 miles, purchased by the Aztec Land and Cattle Company out of the railroad grant lands of the cash-strapped Atlantic and Pacific Railroad at four bits an acre.

The Aztec would be headquartered near a tiny, sleepy and soon to be overwhelmed town named Holbrook. Established ranches in the area were put on notice. Wills were about to be tested by the arival of rough and lawless men with the bark still on, working for a company that didn't mind if the pre-existing and normally peaceful ranchers were put off, out or under.

Things were about to get even more interesting in that country as may be remembered. South of the Aztec range, the Tewksburys tried sheeping-in some of those old-time Texas cowmen who then loudly disagreed, leading to an all-out war in the Pleasant Valley.

We could here note that caught in the middle between that rock of Pleasant Valley and the immovable Aztec was a new ranch at Canyon Creek, carved out of the Mogollon wilderness with nothing but the bare hands and grit of two fearless lads who bore the surname Adams and one slightly older with the same last name as the *pobre vaqueros* just chronicled.

But we'd get ahead of ourselves if we related how even the worst elements of that influx of bad and worse characters were quickly put wise that those boys at Canyon Creek were best left be.

It has been 20 years since we abandoned the Adams bunch - we're past time to catch up.

◆

Part III

Arizona Territory

Brigham City – September, 1881

The wind was chill, but not biting, and blew listlessly from the southwest. Will Adams held Buster on the last rise overlooking what had until recently been his home and pushed his hat back. The moon was full tonight so even though it was a few hours after sunset the landscape was still on display. Some kind of bird – or was it an oversized bat? - darted it's lonely way through the air, wings alternately catching and releasing the moon's light, diving and rearranging its course in an instant to grab food only it could see, unconcerned by Will and Buster's presence.

To the north thunderheads lit up the dark sky with the fingers of God every few seconds. Will paused to watch and wonder. No thunder could be heard, so far away were the billowy-black clouds, but he knew there must be someone nearer who was getting an earful. It was like that this time of year. September thunder storms in northeastern Arizona built all afternoon, drenching whatever was below when they finally broke open. The desert is a fickle mistress – not enough and then too much.

Brigham City was no more – another casualty of the remorseless land. The list of victims was long and distinguished; Brigham City should have felt honored. Instead, a pang pricked Will when he thought of how hard his father, mother and rest of the family had worked in order to make the high desert blossom.

But water is what turns soil into roses and tomatoes and the scarcity makes the country unlivable. Sometimes too much of it does the same thing. The flooding of the Little Colorado in July and August of 1881 washed away their small dams and ditches and, with them, the crops so hard fought and almost ready to harvest.

The family wasn't full of farmers anyway. His father had coaxed crops from the ground back in Iowa and had grown enough to feed themselves every year since then, but the thing they were best at was raising beef cattle. Will couldn't help but feel sorry for the other settlers who lost everything with no backup position.

Just five years earlier, his father, JJ Adams, had arrived in this small valley with his family of eight and instructions from on high to colonize for other Mormon settlers. JJ and Brigham Young had a quiet partnership in the cattle business, so Young himself had summoned JJ from his home in Spring City, Utah to Salt Lake and gave directions personally.

A year later Young was dead, but JJ and his family toiled on in Arizona trying to con the desert into giving up food while they tended their growing herd of cattle. That is until the food washed into the river.

They left the seven foot high protective walls where they had built their homes and moved southeast along the river with the herd to the

131

recently renamed Mormon settlement of Woodruff.

Nathan Tenney and JJ were friends and on good terms - their individual settlements were only a few miles from each other and they were both trying to colonize the area near Holbrook in the Arizona territory. Tenney's settlement had prospered more than JJ's though – at least it hadn't completely flooded out yet.

Will looked down at the two hundred feet of dark and silent walls and wondered how long they would last. His father had asked him to come and recover some hand tools they had left behind when they moved out a few days earlier.

It was late and he was glad he had brought his bedroll. Even though he could imagine ghosts already wandering his former home, he felt comfortable making his bed in front of the massive fireplace. The fire also cheered him and brought back fond memories as fires are wont to do.

Will was by nature an outgoing and happy young man. He stood two inches over six feet with two hundred plus pounds of the lean muscle the times and environment demanded. Born this very day in Sidney, Iowa, he was 22 years old. His parents hadn't mentioned his birthday before he left, but he wasn't bothered. The family had more urgent things to think about.

He took off his gun belt and carefully laid the twin Colt Frontier "Peacemakers" well within reach in case he needed them. Since his father had bought them for him on a previous birthday, a year after they moved to colonize Brigham City, he had never been without them close at hand.

JJ had gone to Salt Lake City to give a report about conditions in northern Arizona to Young's successor, John Taylor. Will could vividly remember that September day after his father's meeting when they walked past the new three-story Zion's Cooperative Mercantile Institution store on main street. There they were in the window arrayed with their gun belt – a more

133

enticing sight to a young man could scarcely be imagined. Well, perhaps one in a dress comes to mind, but be patient – we've got to fetch her all the way from Arkansas.

Samuel Colt had introduced his Single Action Army in 1873. After a spirited competition with Smith & Wesson and their top-break revolver named for Colonel Schofield, the United States Army eventually settled on the Colt design for a variety of reasons, but largely due to its ability to shoot either gun's ammunition.

Colt followed that success with the "Frontier" for the civilian market. Unlike previous cap and ball designs, the new revolver used primed cartridges which made loading much quicker and easier.

The west, being what it was and requiring one to be able to defend oneself, JJ knew the family needed to be better armed as they tried to tame inhospitable land and keep the untamed and un-tameable men at bay.

He also knew Will had been itching for years to have his own revolver after meeting Porter Rockwell a few years before when Rockwell came to their home in Spring City for a secret meeting with JJ. Will was ten at the time, a gangly youth with big hands and even bigger eyes when he saw the heavily bearded legend wearing his Colt Walker.

Being so close to Will's birthday made up JJ's mind. They turned and went into the store and JJ purchased the rig in the window for his son on the spot. An extra dollar bought two boxes of the .44-40 caliber ammunition the guns were chambered for. The guns cost $17.50 each and the day's bill came to an even $40 with the belt. Will wondered where the two double-eagles his father used to pay for the guns came from. Gold or hard money of any kind was scarce as hens teeth.

Will never dreamed he'd have one of the new Colts, much less two. He almost couldn't keep his eyes on the trail as they left Salt Lake and headed for home. The guns felt heavy and substantial and very natural, almost as if he'd been wearing them

135

his whole life. Even though they chaffed after a while from bouncing around on the horse he had no mind to take them off.

Two-gun rigs were becoming more rare. In the days of cap and ball revolvers, which were much more cumbersome and time consuming to reload than the new Colt single actions, many more frontiersmen had two revolvers for the simple reason that ten shots instead of five before reloading were sometimes the difference between keeping your scalp or not. The new ease of reloading had changed much of the need to carry two revolvers.

Not only that but the guns themselves weren't cheap – they each cost about half a months worth of top-hand wages. So more and more cowboys and frontiersmen took to carrying only one on their belt.

That had been more than a ton of lead and many kegs of powder ago. Constant practice enabled him to master those guns as few others could.

Rockwell had let him handle his Walker and aim it those many years ago. Will remembered how hard it was to hold up. Rockwell chuckled at him and told him it was a man's gun and weighed more than four pounds. But then, perhaps sensing something in the boy, Rockwell had shown him how he practiced by shooting at a bank of dirt.

"This way you can see where the ball goes. If you get good enough you can shoot without aiming," he had said. "The trick is not to shoot fast, but smart. Any tin horn can waste lead but very few men can keep their wits an' shoot straight when folks is shootin' back at 'em.

"Plus, you can go dig yer lead outa the dirt an' melt 'er down ag'in."

They had walked into a gully by the Adams house and the old man showed Will what he meant. Shot after shot went just where Ol' Port intended. Sometimes it was hard to see through the clouds of black powder smoke, but the tin cans they had brought for targets consistently danced high into the air or were kept rolling. Will learned some tricks about revolvers that day.

Rockwell's last piece of advice was something Will remembered his entire life after: "Son, if ya ever put on a gun don't never take it off when yer out a doors an' have it handy when yer under-roof. It's gotta become part a ya cause ya never know when you'll need it. Keep it close."

In later years Will would find it was better to take off his revolvers when working cattle, but rarely was he seen without them otherwise.

He also remembered how when they got back to the house Rockwell had carefully cleaned and reloaded the huge revolver with five shots and let the hammer rest on the empty chamber.

"So's I don't shoot my durn foot off carryin' it," he chuckled. "I load up six fer practice or if'n I think thar's gonna be warlike situations, but only five if I'm plannin' on bein' peaceable or travlin'."

◆

It had been in this very room a few months earlier that a worn out and discouraged gold and copper miner had stopped at Brigham City on his way back home to Virginia. He admired Will's gun rig and asked if he had seen the new Winchester. Will said he'd heard of them, but hadn't been able to hold or shoot one yet. The old miner rolled out his bedroll and there in the middle was what looked like a brand new rifle. It was chambered for the same .44-40 caliber his revolvers took.

The miner laughed when he saw the look on Will's face. "I figured you might like that thar. It's a '73 carbine I bought a few years back when I thunk I might was gonna hafta fight off claim jumpers. Never did get a claim good enough ta jump, so's it's been used precious little.

"Injuns been purty much cleaned out 'twixt here an' Virginny an' I'm not gonna need it back on the family farm. I'm a wonderin' if'n we might not make a deal on 'er."

Will had jumped at the chance and when the dickering was finally done, he had himself a fine, almost new, $30 Winchester in exchange for three brand-new shirts his mom had made to trade at Tenney's store and an older cap and ball Remington his father hadn't used for several years.

Gun-wise, Will was now about as set as a man could get in 1881. Very few cowboys had one of the newer carbines and fewer still packed one on their horse most places. His '73 rode in a saddle scabbard on the left side of Buster so that it didn't interfere with him shaking out a loop. At first it had been an adjustment, but within a few weeks he got used to it being there. It was now part of his "rig" and unless he was working stock hard or "brush popping" he kept it right where he could get to it easily.

◆

The next morning Will pointed Buster towards Woodruff before the sun was up. They stopped and gazed back again on Brigham City. It was too bad they had to leave it, but he knew all things happen for their own reason and was excited about the possibilities to come.

His older brother John Quincy and he were thinking about heading southwest a ways and scouting locations for a ranch they could homestead in the mountains around the Mogollon Rim. Will was looking forward to the hard work and rewards of building a ranch of their own.

Edge would be going along as well. Since they had all grown up together, he and John Q considered him to be their oldest brother and idolized everything he did. He was a quiet man of 32 now, still sparing of the spoken word.

But he was hell on wheels with his single Colt, slung low and kept tied down. Even rough characters shied away and left him alone. He and Will frequently practiced together - if there was anyone who could keep up to Will's guns it would be Edge.

He'd been 12 years old before uttering any word around the family. Will had mostly fuzzy memories at that age, but the first time Edge spoke stood out in his mind.

The family had moved from the hills by Fairfield north to the beautiful Cache Valley on the Utah and Idaho border where Young also owned land which was much more suitable to raising cattle.

"James an' me hasn't had no taters yet, John Q. Pass 'em this way, would ya?" JJ said one evening as the family sat at supper.

Edge piped up out of the blue: "My name's not James, it's Edge. Bellows." His face had an expression that was a combination of embarrassment and defiance, but those features softened when he saw the amazement on Mary's face.

Her eyes teared up as she smiled. Everyone else just stared at him.

A complete silence lasted for about a five count until Mary jumped up from her place, ran around the table and hugged him tightly.

"Oh my boy! I *never* thought to hear your sweet voice! My prayers have been answered!"

All at once everyone was talking except for Will, who screeched with delight without knowing quite why, and little Martha, who just watched and made a mess of her food while mother's attention was diverted.

"Didya say yore name was Edge, son?"

"Yep."

"Ah knew ya'd talk when ya got good n' ready."

Nod.

"Do you want to be called by James or Edge?" Mary asked.

"Edge."

"Ya got any kinfolk ya know of?"

Head shakes no.

"Didya say Bellows?"

Nod.

"Ah think ah heard tell of a Bellows down south a where we come from in Ioway."

No reply.

"How come it took ya so long ta talk?" asked John Q innocently, with admiring eyes that said if

Edge didn't want to talk there must have been a very good reason.

Silence returned abruptly while they waited for the answer – even Martha paused throwing her mashed potatoes on the floor.

Edge looked thoughtfully at them all.

"Guess I jes din't need ta say nothin'," he finally said.

A long moment passed before JJ roared with laughter; everyone including Edge joined in. Martha agreed by heaving her tiny spoon at Will's nose.

Edge's self-imposed silence was broken.

That had been almost 20 years ago. Will smiled at the memory, reined Buster to the south and rode off with a light heart.

Woodruff – September, 1882

The Nathan Lee Smith wagon moved slowly through the dry desert just a few miles north of Woodruff. Every time they had to cross a sandy arroyo they slowed even more. The oxen labored mightily even though there were four of them.

The trek from Salt Lake had taken almost five weeks. This was after the three months for the trip to get to Salt Lake City from Winter Quarters, Nebraska in the first place and the three months journey to Winter Quarters from Arkansas.

Soon after arriving in Salt Lake, Smith had been summoned to the Bishop's office for an interview. He had been asked about but confessed no knowledge of any relation to the Smith family of the Mormon church. He related the story of how he and his wife, Bonnie, had been baptized many years before.

Nathan and his family of six were from Des Arc, Arkansas. One March day in 1857, a very persuasive man had come to stay for a time by the name of Parley Pratt who ended up convincing Nathan to join his church.

The prairie country of Arkansas was news-starved and so the Smith's had barely ever heard of the Mormon church or the infamous Smith family. They had all gathered in the Jones home, who lived nearby and where Pratt was staying, to hear what he had to say.

The upshot was both families had joined the church by being baptized in the nearby White river. When Pratt left he put Nathan in charge of the little "branch" which consisted of the four adults and the two young Jones children. They took turns meeting every Sunday at each others home and reading from the one Book of Mormon they had bought from Pratt.

They never heard from Pratt again and did not know he had been murdered only a few months after leaving Des Arc, just outside Van Buren, Arkansas, about 80 miles away. Neither did they hear from any church leaders at all since no one knew of their existence after Pratt was killed. But they continued to practice what they had been taught and what they learned from reading their copy of the Book of Mormon. Unsure of the proper authority, the children had never been baptized.

William and Martha Jones had two children by 1857, but Martha died in 1860 from complications of her third pregnancy at only 27 years of age. William's second wife, a dark-haired beauty named Francis, died just five years later from what the Smiths believed were the very hard living conditions experienced in Arkansas during the civil war. She was married at 16 and dead at 21.

William's third wife, Abigail, gave him a daughter and son before she too died in 1876. William passed away just two years later at the age of 40 from pneumonia, officially, but the Smiths always thought he gave up from pure and simple heartbreak.

After William's death the Smiths took the four orphaned Jones children, which included 16 year-old William, 13 year-old Mattie, eight year-old Domer, and six year-old James, into their home. It was the way of such things in those times and Nathan and Bonnie Smith were only too happy to oblige since they were childless and had known the Jones children all their lives.

Even a decade and a half later life never quite returned to Des Arc what it had been before the war. The Jones children stayed on with the Smiths and in 1881 Nathan decided to sell the farm, pack up everything that remained and move to Salt Lake City where they had heard the Mormons were making the Great Basin into a modern day Eden.

Bishop Johnson related how Pratt had been murdered shortly after departing Des Arc, leaving the two families possibly the last people Pratt ever converted.

He also told Nathan about a new farming community in Arizona that had been settled especially for other Mormons looking for land.

He asked if Nathan and his family would be willing to make another relatively short trip to Woodruff in the northern Arizona Territory. Smith explained that they were nearly out of provisions, but Johnson said they could be resupplied for the trip from the storehouse.

The Brady Davis family had also been getting ready to leave for Arizona and Bishop Johnson suggested they should go together for protection. Smith was sure his sturdy oxen would be able to finish the trip.

And so it was that day in 1882 found the Smith wagon with the four Jones children and the Davis wagon with their two sets of identical twins a few short miles from their destination of Woodruff. Domer Jones was 12 years old.

◆

All morning Will had been practicing alone. The naturally dark earth in the bluffs north of town made an excellent spot to shoot. Rockwell's advice from years before had not fallen on deaf ears – as always, Will could see exactly where every shot hit.

He could shoot equally well with either hand. He kept both eyes open because it made finding the target much easier. He didn't even have to aim since he had taught himself to point shoot. He was very accurate – so much so, in fact, he had won several shooting competitions and was beginning to make a name for himself with his two Colt revolvers. It was widely thought no one around could out-shoot Will Adams unless it was his older brother, Edge.

People marveled at the amount of black powder, ingots of lead and boxes of primers that came to Woodruff from Salt Lake City on a regular basis. Will was frequently out in the bluffs practicing with Edge whenever they got the opportunity. When it wasn't live ammunition, they drove Mary crazy at home with their incessant cocking and firing with guns unloaded, practice they called "dry firing". They competed with each other to see who could cock their gun and squeeze the trigger five times the fastest.

"I'm not sure which'll wear out first – those guns or my nerves," Mary frequently told JJ.

If it wasn't dry firing, they spent many enjoyable evenings reloading their brass cases with the special pliers-like Ideal tool they had purchased mail order from back east. It was an arduous task melting the lead and carefully pouring it into the bullet mold on the end of the tool and then knocking it out once it had cooled, but it saved a lot of money.

A .44-40 cartridge cost about two cents, but by reloading their own Will and Edge could get the cost down to less than half a cent each. In a time of very little cash money, reloading was an absolute necessity for anyone who shot as much as they did.

Years of such practice had made them very good and extremely fast. Will could empty both guns by shooting at two different targets five times each in less than four seconds, hitting the cans each time he fired. He would cock both guns at the same time and pull each trigger within a hair of each other so the two shots sounded almost like one. People who hadn't seen him do it usually didn't believe until they had. And even then they weren't sure their own eyes hadn't played tricks on them.

Edge only carried one of the Colt revolvers, but he was every bit as fast and accurate as his little brother. Edge had stayed home that day to tend some leather that needed fixing on his saddle.

Riding back from the bluffs Will felt on top of the world. He never tired of the view in the clear desert air. The ghostly purple of the distant mountains gave way to progressively darker and then more subtle shades of blue and turquoise around the Mogollon rim. Closer, greens and tans mixed until deeper browns and distinct reds added their hues from an enchanted palette worthy of the Master painter.

But the desert was as treacherous as it was beautiful. Creatures better left alone frequently slithered their patient way in search of sustenance.

One such, six inches thick and as many feet long, venom to rattles, lay dozing in the tall, tan grass between wagon ruts, its blood warmed by the sun. Practically invisible without movement and deadly quick, awakened by the smallest vibration, it could not fail to miss the approach of a thousand pounds of horse and rider.

Traversing such landscape it's not overly wise to daydream, but Will drank in the day-dreamy vista. Who would not in his place?

There's an extra sense that develops in those who live in harsh environs. Just below the surface of consciousness it lurks, forever making use of the other senses to discern danger, calculate escape angles and constantly adjusting for new realities, all in the unthinking part of the brain until activated by need. An instant was all it took to awaken fully in Will.

A warning rattle, a high side-stepping horse, a rider nonpareil and attuned - a lesser horseman would have been thrown on the very top of the threat – not so this one. Away skittered mount and man on a new path directly toward the distant Atlantic Ocean, the dangerous serpent having been given the west side of the road and gladly. All would have been well except the immediate way east led directly over a rather steep arroyo bank.

Down plunged horse and rider, dodging through cacti and sotol and sage in bloom. Will leaned far back over his horse's straining rump, becoming as horizontal as he could without getting the back of his head beaten in by flying hooves. Soon it became evident horse and rider were transformed to horse and passenger, but still the passenger kept to his precarious seat.

At the bottom were two rarities of the desert – the first, a massive and ancient cottonwood which could only exist there because of the other, a several feet-deep natural rock spring. The tree stretched its thick branches in every direction, one of which being a little above riding-head-height and directly over the unintended path of the hurtling centaur.

With only a quick impulse and scarcely a wisp of conscious thought, Will made his dismount in the most advantageous way available during one of his horse's upstrokes by kicking free of the stirrups and clinging to said branch as Buster continued on in the general direction of the sea and out from under him. It was an incredible performance worthy of a circus.

But the god of the horseman is whimsical, giving with a smile and taking back with a laugh. For a few seconds Will swung precariously from the branch like a monkey in boots until he had the returning sense to realize he couldn't long grasp a tree limb of that diameter and dropped unceremoniously onto his feet and thence to his seat into the pool below. His hat was gone and his guns and clothes were wet, but his sense of humor was intact. He laughed at his good fortune to be alive and still in one piece.

He waggled one boot tip above the water and then the other. He looked at each arm and noted they both still had hands at the ends of them. The fingers on the hands wiggled. Knees and elbows

155

bent in the correct direction. He could swivel his neck just fine and...that's when he noticed he was not alone.

The Smith and Davis families had stopped in the shade of the desert behemoth for lunch and were partly through when the spectacle of Will and Buster burst over the top of the arroyo and into their lives. Neither had previously known of the existence of the other. The assembled crowd's amazement was universal, Will's none the less. They stared at each other for a few moments, the only sounds the soft gurgle of water and other returning noises after Nature's held breath.

"Howdy!" said Will, eyes lingering on pretty Domer for an instant longer than might be considered quite proper. Disheveled and soaking he may have been – he was still a young man.

"Umm, errrr, howdy," said Nathan.

"Are you hurt at all? Get up out of that water!" cried Bonnie, her motherly instinct replacing shock.

Brady Davis just sat there munching a sandwich, shaking his head and chuckling to himself while his wife, Shelter, had kind of a rueful smile on her face too. Their two sets of twins, one boys and the other girls, just stared.

"Oh - no, I'm not hurt much. Lost my hat somewhere's an' I'll have ta clean these guns purty soon, but hurt, no, not much." He looked himself over again as if to make sure.

"You get on up outa there this instant!" Bonnie repeated, becoming a little testy at the nonchalant manner of the soaked horseman.

As he obediently rose, water rivuleting everywhere, Will spied Buster - his horse had been stopped down the arroyo a ways when loose reins had become entangled in the fork of a convenient greasewood trunk.

A horseman minus his horse is a mere man, so he tromped off to retrieve his mount. The families watched with interest as he slogged through the centuries-deep sand and returned with the now *mancito* animal.

"Is your horse okay?" Nathan asked as Will tied Buster to one of the rear wagon wheels.

157

"Aw, he's 'bout as good as he ever gets, I s'pose. What a snake!"

"He looks like a nice horse - ya shouldn't call him that," Domer spoke up for the first time.

Will surveyed the crowd and found them all in general agreement with this sentiment.

"Naw, he's not the snake, although he does slither friskily aroun' sometimes in the mornin's jes fer fun. The snake was up on top on the wagon road an' why Buster an' me are now down here with you-all. Bigger 'round than my arm looked like, an' meaner than a badger with a sore tooth. Buster was wise ta leave that locale, yes he was. Onny wished I could'a stayed on 'im!" This discourse delivered with a self-deprecating grin.

"That's just nonsense, young man. I've never seen better riding in all my born days. You come over here and set yourself down while I fix you up sumthin' to eat," replied Bonnie, bustling about as she spoke.

"I second that motion about the riding," Brady added with a nod to Will.

"Thankee, sir. I figure it'd probly be a good idear ta pour some little water outa both muh boots an' guns," Will said, sitting on a convenient exposed root. "I'll hafta load these rounds all over ag'in in muh belt – won't do ta have wet powder an' primers."

He noticed young James staring at his guns as he removed the cartridges and wiped them down. "How old are ya, little man? What's yer name?"

"James. I'm ten"

"Waal, yer jes of an age when Ol' Port showed me howta shoot. Ya ever done much shootin', James?"

"No, he hasn't," Nathan said. "We don't have a lot in the way of guns. Just a Stevens scatter gun and a cut-down Springfield rifle. Powder is dear – every shot we make has gotta count."

"Thet's shore 'nuff true. Jes this morning I was out practicing with these revolvers an' used up purty much all muh ammo 'cept fer what was on muh belt an' in muh guns. Now thet's no good an' I still got ta make it home alive. Man out here alone without a ready gun could be in a world a

159

trouble, brother. Lucky I still got muh '73 full-up on the saddle. Where y'all headed an' where've ya come from? Them oxen look plumb wore-out."

"We're headed for the settlement at Woodruff."

"Are ya now! Y'all Mormon immigrants or sumthin'? Most ever-body ta Woodruff is."

Bonnie handed him down a sandwich stealing a warning glance at her husband. "You are just full of questions and that's a fact," she said. Will noticed her unease and guessed the reason.

"Don't be shy, ma'am. Reckon I'm one too. I know thar's folks 'round don't take kindly ta us. What with the Marshalls trying ta find anyone who's got more'n one or three wives, or bushwackers out ta collect a bounty, it's got so's ya can't put one foot in front a the other without steppin' on a snake!" He chuckled at that. "Maybe thet was a Marshall up on the wagon track," winking at Domer, who blushed and looked away.

"Anyhow, I live over ta Woodruff now, so I kin take y'all in with me if ya want." Will looked at Nathan and then smiled at Bonnie again. "This sammich shore eats good, ma'am. My name is Will Adams an' well pleased ta meet y'all."

"I'm Nathan Smith and this is my wife, Ma Bonnie. That oldest one there is William, then that'n is Mattie, the shy one is Domer and you already met James. That's the Davis family, Brady, his wife Shelter and their children. They've been with us since Salt Lake City. We'd be happy to have your company on the trip into town, Will. Thankee."

"Y'all got two sets a twins an' both identical?" Will asked. Shelter nodded. "Well, I'll be! Thet's gotta be a chance in a million! Never heerd tell a such a thing."

"Do ya have three wives? I never heard tell a such a thing, either!" said Domer with less than completely innocent eyes and not quite as shy as advertised.

"Domer! You mind what you say," Ma Bonnie scolded.

Will laughed again, tugging on a boot. "Why no ma'am, I don't. I ain't been able ta throw a loop on even a first one yet!"

"Oh, is *thet* how ya catch 'em out here?"

Brady Davis chuckled again.

"That'll be quite enough of that talk, the both a ya. Mattie and Domer, help me get this lunch cleaned up and loaded so's we can be on our way."

◆

It didn't take long for the wagons to be repacked or for the little bunch to arrive in Woodruff. Several people came out onto their porches in the late afternoon sun to wave at Will and wonder over the two families he had in tow.

The makeshift party pulled up at Tenney's General Store. Will got down and made introductions all around. When the townsfolk heard both families had come down from Salt Lake City they all wanted to know the latest news. What was the mood? Who had the Marshalls arrested?

Nathan Tenney put a stop to more questions and showed Smith and Davis where they could unhitch and stow their wagons and oxen.

"The rest of y'all come on in here an' ya kin settle in the back room 'til we kin he'p ya git set up an' build homes fer yersefs."

Mrs. Tenney, who was used to taking in new settlers this way, soon had them all as comfortable as they could be in the space available.

The following months found the Smiths and Davis' moved onto their own farm plots and into smallish dugout homes the entire community helped them to erect.

◆

Fast slid past the seasons as JJ and the boys rode the range and tended their growing cattle herd. They rapidly gained a well-deserved reputation of being a family of qualified stockmen. It was obvious they were much better at it than farming.

The Little Colorado flooded again which took its toll of the Woodruff community. The Adams boys decided it was time to move to that fertile valley they had scouted a few years back to begin their own spread. John Q had gotten married the year before and he and Will figured it was high time they had their own ranch. Edge was chomping at the bit.

Will and Domer Jones had kept up a friendly repartee over the years as she grew into a lovely young woman just a year shy of sweet. Most evenings found Will at the Smith household helping out where he could but more generally making a nuisance of himself.

Ma Bonnie knew only too well why he was there as did Domer and everyone else in town. Knowing smiles were exchanged whenever they were seen together. Even Will's shooting practice took a back seat to Domer sometimes, much to the chagrin of Edge.

JJ and Mary moved again to settle yet another piece of the Arizona wilderness, but one far enough away from the Little Colorado so they couldn't be flooded out. They had shifted the still growing herd southwest about 30 miles, to just north of the Rim. The new settlement was dubbed Adams Valley, but later the name was changed to Wilford.

No sooner was the family firmly ensconced than did the boys make their final plans for starting their own spread where the water mixed clean and cold between the Mule and Canyon creeks.

◆

"So y'all are jes up an' leavin, ag'in? Jes like thet? Wilford wasn't fur 'nuff 'way from me fer ya, huh? When ya ever plannin' on seein' me ag'in, Will Adams? You'll be beyond the rim fer months at a time, no doubt." Domer looked Will straight in the face.

165

He shuffled back and forth. He squirmed. He felt sweat running between his shoulder blades. Were people supposed to sweat on their back that way? Other wonderings flashed across his poor overloaded mind – anything to keep it off the dervish in front of him and her too-direct questions. She stood, hands on hips – shapely hips he noticed for the thousandth time – and stared up at him without an inch of mercy in her manner.

"Is this 'spose ta be some sorta half-baked 'pology an' goodbye? Yer brother gits married an' now ya tell me yer gonna be their third wheel in a ranch thet don't even exist? I do sometimes wonder if there's a brain at work 'tween those ears a-yers or not." Her drawl thickened in corellation to her temper.

"Aw, it's not like thet an' ya know it. 'Sides, Edge's goin' too." The dull ox struggles, miring itself deeper.

"An' I'm supposed ta jes sit here doin' heaven knows what while yer off cowboyin' beyond the rim? Don't ya think thar might be some little chance a brighter an' better lookin' fella might not come 'long an' sweep me away? But yer not worried 'bout thet cause yer trying ta git rid 'o me, ain't ya!"

"Now wait jes a minute...." Will was cut off as if he hadn't even spoken.

"I may only be 15, but thet doesn't mean I'm gonna be stayin' right here in Woodruff forever. Ya jes think on thet fer awhile, Will Adams."

Without another word she flounced off to the front door of their little home and was gone. Yes, flounced is decidedly the word. Will looked about half a mind to go after her, but he hadn't even talked to Mr. Smith about her hand in marriage yet.

The evening had not gone as planned at all. He'd never seen her so worked up and couldn't figure why she was. After all, he was only going a few miles away to try to start a ranch he could bring her to, rather than asking her to rough it with all of them until they made it a go. Wasn't that the gentlemanly thing to do?

James came out, sat beside him and grinned. "She's madder'n a wet hen, I'd say. Ya gonna marry her an' make it all better?" James was a very perceptive 13 year-old. He and Will had become close with all of the shooting Edge and Will had taught him. James didn't have a gun yet so he used one of Will's. He was a good shooter in his own right.

"I dunno. Somehow everything's gotten mixed up an' out a order."

"Upside down is how ma told it the other day."

"Yep – upside down is about it! I've been throwed off an' I know I gotta git back on but durned if I kin find a stirrup!" Will shook his head and chuckled.

James laughed too. "Ya best not let Domer hear ya talkin' 'bout stirrups 'round *her*!"

They talked the Seven Sisters half a circle in the western sky, but James's sister never reappeared.

Holbrook – July, 1884

Cass Bellows was riding drag on the immense herd of Texas longhorns, eating dust and cussing luck. They'd been on Aztec lands for better than 100 miles, but still they pushed the cattle almost due west.

Longhorns were out of the ordinary in this country – they had driven past many small ranches which were running mostly white-face cattle. Cass wondered why they kept on. The boss said these ranchers would have to move soon or late – why not now?

Still, this was the big herd so Cass figured they were moving closer to the headquarters with more room. The thought didn't make the dust go down any easier.

His saddle partner was a man named Andy Cooper, another supposed Texas bad man. Cooper wasn't his real name – it was Bullins or Blemans or something like that, but Cass couldn't remember and didn't care. They'd been paired

169

together because the trail boss thought they were alike – trouble-men good with guns.

But Cass was indifferent at best about Andy. He was lazy and not anything like a good cowboy. He kept running his mouth about how he was going to find a nice spread so he could squat on it and send for the rest of his family back in Texas. The Hashknife drive was just a means to an Arizona ranch end for Cooper.

In some ways, Andy reminded him of his brother Dirk. Cass sighed. *No, Dirk on his worst day'd make ten Andy Coopers*, he thought.

Loose shale on top of solid stone, a shod hoof skidding, an over-balanced horse and down they go. Dirk probably would have only had a leg mashed if it wasn't for the unnatural angle his head had struck the rock shelf. Just like that his light had fled. Cass knew it the moment he saw the mess. Never should have been in the saddle across that big rock. But that was Dirk.

And that was the desert west – it had a thousand, thousand ways of leaving a body behind you never figured on.

Cass sighed again, thinking about it. He'd grieved for as long as the circumstances afforded, buried Dirk where the wind blew free in the springtime, bending the grass to the east, then he and Bryant had started the bunch again for the west and the promise of high New Mexico pastures.

Indians had gotten Mays two weeks later. He and Mays had left the herd, running as far and fast as they could to no avail. Bryant had given the Apaches all they could handle for the better part of two days holed up behind his wrecked wagon. But in the end they came upon him after he ran out of rounds for his Winchester. Even then two more braves died - one from Mays using the rifle as a club and the last from his Bowie knife - before the remainder wrestled him to the ground, took their bloody trophy and watched him die while he cursed them and their ancestors.

Cass never understood why the Apaches left him alone - after killing Mays they simply vanished, taking the cattle. He'd buried Bryant by caving a wash of sand over him as best he could

171

for the Apaches had looted the wagon and ridden off with all they could carry including both of their shovels. It was a hell of an end for another good man, Cass thought.

But the Indians hadn't found the gold. He and Dirk had saved the original five double eagles from their farm sale back in St. Jo's. They had never divvied them up although the year passed and neither of their brothers had shown up. Dirk hadn't mentioned it again even through his tormented times.

When they decided on their drive, Cass suggested they use it for emergency money, so they inlaid them in the bottom part of the wagon covered with an old piece of wood. Now Cass had them sewn into his pants.

He looked around at the mountain majesty and had to smile. It was just such a place they had wanted to find. Maybe he'd scout around with Cooper and latch onto something. Suddenly he felt unaccountably good – like the world was smiling on him. He had no reason to, but there it was nonetheless.

172

Wilford / Canyon Creek – June, 1885

Splitting their time between JJ's new settlement of Wilford and their homesteaded acreage approximately eight miles south, the three men had their hands full.

As the crow flies, the distance from Wilford to the confluence of the Mule and Canyon creeks was only eight miles – but up, down and around just about doubled it. For Wilford was on the north and Canyon Creek to the south of a tremendous natural barrier called the Mogollon Rim. Between them stood buttresses of soaring cliffs and drop-offs sheer as to boggle the mind.

At the ranch the work was all they imagined and more. From before first light until well after last they toiled. The immensity of the task would have been its own detriment but not for the single-mindedness of the men who did it. They proceeded from one job to another until the whole of it dwindled to a size which could at least be comprehended.

173

The house came first – there was no shortage of trees from which to shape walls. It was erected by the three working together in just two weeks. It wasn't a structure intended for permanency nor was it fancy. One square room, twenty feet on a side, was all they started with, fully intending to replace and augment when time permitted.

A small barn and adjoining corrals came next. The term 'rawhide' might have been invented for describing this outfit, but they forced the wilderness grandeur into habitability and what would become a beautiful ranch, bit by bit, slowly grew from nothing.

Their animals fared well on the lush mountain pasture and crystal water. Hunting was nowhere better with natural beauty sufficient to blind the eye ever in view. Of such was made the first ranch at Canyon Creek.

All the while Will thought of Domer. He worked hard enough for two men, his minds-eye rehearsing the scene of her first arrival as his wife at their mountain retreat. He could see just how it would go and it gave him purpose. He was a happy and content young man with a glorious future planned. She would finally see and understand why he had waited until he got things just so; all for her.

He was sure she would regret her hasty words at their last parting. The thought made him smile.

Woodruff – August, 1885

The Davis party consisted of the two wagons of Brady and Shelter, their two sets of identical twins, the Johnson clan with his two wives and ten children spread between three wagons, and four more wagons carrying the entire Jorgenson family of the two patriarch brothers, their wives and a combined seventeen-strong brood; all with the attendant oxen, horses, cattle, milch cows, squealing pigs and bleating goats. They would make a dust that could be seen for miles.

Oh, and we forgot to mention two other passengers – Domer Jones and her brother James were riding along with the Davis family. The

Smiths were staying in Arizona so Brady and Shelter unofficially adopted the two.

Will had not been to see her since that night. She kept her feelings inside so as not to embarrass herself as she had that fateful evening. He'd thrown her over, hadn't he? In her secret heart she knew it wasn't true, but her womanly pride wouldn't allow it to be admitted openly.

"I can't believe yer not at least sendin' word down to Wilford! I know sure's I'm sittin' here Will would not want ya to go 'fore he had a chance to talk to ya." James knew it was a mistake and didn't hesitate to tell his sister – but she was a stubborn girl.

"An' I wonder if yer ever shuttin' up about thet! Mercy, James, I can't hep it if he figures ta be off alone ruther than fetch me with 'im. He knows how I feel an' he had his chance! Now hush. An' I ferbid ya sneakin' around ta tell 'im yerself!"

Since the decision had been made for her and James to go with the Davis family to Mexico, she'd not seen Will. She had written him two letters, both of which ended up in the fire. She knew what her heart felt, but she didn't dare put it in writing for Will to laugh at. She couldn't bare her feelings to him that way again unless she was sure he felt the same.

She vowed he'd have to come to her this time - if he came at all. Would he? She'd be in another country, after all, 300 miles away maybe before he even knew she had left.

It'd serve him right. She imagined his dismay at finding her gone and wishing he hadn't been such a brainless fool. It made her smile.

But as they rolled and bumped their tortuous way south, she began to wonder if she was doing the right thing. Would she see Will again? What did her future hold? A pang of remorse swept her with overpowering intensity. She forcefully put it aside in its own special box - locked away against the day they'd re-meet. She *would* see him. She knew she would. The thought made her smile for a second time.

Nathan Tenney watched them go sadly –
Davis and Johnson were solid men, but the
Jorgensons had recently arrived from Denmark
and from what he had seen were no good match
for the country and dangers they'd have to face.
He didn't expect to hear a good report.

Canyon Creek Ranch – June, 1886

It had been a long trip. Leaving Mary, John
Quincy's wife, and Edge in Wilford at their
parents abandoned ranch house, both Will and
John Q had headed north to Salt Lake City for a
special conference with Mormon Church
authorities on local conditions. They'd been
asked to pack up and move their cattle herd south
to Mexico to help establish the fledgling colonies
there.

JJ's settlement of Wilford was both beautiful
and dangerous. More and more Texas Hashknife
cowboys from the Aztec crowded in with them.
They always pushed. Cabins built by the original

settlers, but abandoned for various reasons would be taken up by those cowboys or claimed by the Aztec. Even though the land around Wilford was not technically on Aztec purchases, the vast ranch pretty much surrounded it and controlled the entire area.

Finally, as their position became more untenable, JJ decided to move his herd and family to Mexico. He had been urged to do so before, but was understandably reluctant to have to reestablish himself yet again. He wasn't a polygamist, but his fate seemed to be tied to those friends of his who were. The difficult decision was not made overnight, but over many sleepless nights and numerous family councils with John Q, Will and Edge.

And Will missed Domer. He still had trouble thinking she had left that way. Not even a word of goodbye. Had he misjudged her that badly?

Neither of the Adams boys were overly thrilled about leaving the work they had started on their own ranch. Even though their father had moved south to the colonies nine months before,

179

they felt their ranch was far enough away from the trouble that it might pass them by. So far, the Aztec cowboys had stayed pretty much north of the Rim and they'd been left alone on Canyon Creek.

Will had to admit to himself he wanted to go mostly because of Domer. John Q favored staying at Canyon Creek, but Will was for pushing south. They still hadn't come to a final decision. Edge, as usual, kept his own counsel.

John Q drove the wagon with Mary beside him filled with the provisions they would need for the coming months ahead of pulling out for Wilford and thence onto the long trek south if that proved to be what they decided. Will rode ahead on Blue, Edge beside him on Jasper.

As they halted at the final precipice of the rim, Edge's keen eyes were first to see something that put a worry in all of them – smoke curled from their chimney pipe in the valley thousands of feet below.

"Thet don' seem right," he observed in his quiet way.

Will nodded. "Ya know, Quince, I think Edge'n me'll jes meander on down thar fer a look-see. Ya come perambulatin' 'long when ya kin, an' make sure's ya come loaded. I don't like the looks a thet thar."

"Easy now, Will. Don't be burnin' yore bridges 'fore ya git to 'em," his big brother cautioned.

Will laughed. "Yer metaphors is showin' a mix thet don't make no sense. 'Sides, I'm allays careful 'bout what I burn - but thar shore shouldn't be nuthin' burnin' in thet house right now!"

He and Edge spurred ahead to start the scramble it took to get to their valley far below.

◆

The trip down to the flat took the two men longer than they would have liked though they passed in record time.

They paused at the tree line to take stock of the situation. Smoke curled lazily over the house under a cloudless sun. Any other time that would

181

be a welcoming sight, but now it appeared somehow sinister. The feeling that a stranger was partaking of all their hard work made Will boil inside.

Edge's horse stamped impatiently.

"Whachu thinkin'?"

Will hadn't moved so intently was he studying the scene. Their place was half a mile from where they sat their horses. He pulled first one Colt and then the other and loaded the last chamber in each, leaving the hammers on half-cock and re-holstering.

"I'm thinkin' someone decided they could squat inter our house an' I don't like 'er one bit. Probly some dang Aztecs. Ya know they allays wanted ta git their greedy paws on Canyon Crick."

"Yup. Waal, ya done talked 'er ta death. Le's go git 'em out." Edge moved his horse forward at a brisk walk having already loaded his sixth as well. Will chuckled grimly at Edge and followed.

They still hadn't seen further sign of anyone besides the smoke and the strange horses in the corrals. As they approached they grew more careful. Edge felt eyes on him.

A long rifle shot from their front door they pulled up and watched. Nothing moved. Both dismounted, keeping their horses between them and the silent house.

"Shore is quiet," Will said.

"You wanna haloo 'em or jes go on in thar?" Edge wondered.

"I reckon we oughter be friendly 'til we know better." Yelling then, "Haloo the house! Anybody ta home?"

"Why shore we are, stranger," a voice from inside spoke up. "Y'all jes come on closer if yer peaceable. Not many vis'tors we get up in these parts."

Will and Edge walked their horses closer, still on their guard. "Whose house is this?" asked Will.

"It be our'n. An' who be ye?"

"I'm Will Adams an' this here's muh brother, Edge. Mind if we come up on the porch?"

183

"Come ahead. I heerd a ye. Ya got a ranch 'round these parts, doncha?" The door opened and Andy Cooper walked out followed by Cass Bellows both holding Winchesters at their sides.

"Ya might say thet," said Will with a slight grin.

Cooper was immediately wary. "Whar 'bouts y'all have yore place?"

"Yer standin' on the porch, pard." Edge spoke for the first time.

Cass glanced at Andy. Andy looked a little surprised but not overly. "Well, now, boys. This here's my main side-partner, Cass. Him an' me been doin' a lot o' scoutin' back o' this country. This place been vacant for weeks – we fig'red it ta be 'bandoned."

When Cooper had mentioned Cass's name Edge looked at him sharply and found Cass looking right back. Something very familiar was in the air.

Will hadn't noticed the undercurrent. "I kin tell ya right now it ain't been abandoned. We was off ta Salt Lake an' now we come back with supplies

184

enough ta carry right on with what we were about. Them's our stock what roams 'round thet we din't git rounded up ta take ta Wilford while we were gone. Thet's muh other brother John Q an' his wife in the wagon, yonder."

"All we got is yer word fer it, stranger."

"Naw. Ya got my word fer it too." Something about the way Edge said it put a chill in the air - as if he was just waiting for an excuse to throw his gun. Cooper wasn't at all sure he could get his long gun into action quicker than this quiet stranger. He wasn't about to take the chance. He'd heard of the salty characters south of the Rim.

"Now, jes hold up thar. Les' discuss this a bit 'fore we all go ta hell an' leather." Cooper was liking none of this situation which had quickly grown out of his control. If ever he had seen righteous indignation in two faces it was here. He didn't so much mind being in the wrong as bucking a deck he knew might be stacked against him.

Edge continued, looking back at Cass, dismissing Cooper as insignificant. "He said yer

185

name was Cass. He din't mention another name. Ya got one?"

Cass smiled. The first clue had been the name - he'd figured out the familiarity while Edge was speaking. "I shore do. My brothers an' I went by the name a 'Bellows' back in Missouri. An' thet's the name I still use."

The expression on Edge's face never changed an iota. He slowly walked towards Cass. In the silence Cooper wondered what on earth was going on. Will figured it out at 'Bellows'. Edge got in front of Cass and looked him straight in the eye.

"You was the last one waved at me when me an' pa left thet mornin'. I 'member it like it was yastidy."

And then a strange thing happened, something Will had never seen Edge do with anyone in more than 20 years – he threw a huge bear hug around his older brother Cass who returned it every bit as strong, everything else forgotten.

Will's eyebrows and jaw went different directions. He looked away out of respect.

186

Cooper was not so cool. "What in ternation is goin' on? Ya know each other, Cass?"

The trance was broken. Edge had a bigger smile on his face than Will had ever seen before. Cass had shiny eyes.

"Why shore ya mule-eared ijut! This is muh baby brother Edge who I never laid eyes on from the time he was a youngster ta this very now! I fig'red all this time he been dead an' gone."

◆

The tension sort of oozed out of the situation after that. Edge and Cass went off to the corral together talking animatedly. At least Cass was – Edge never got overly dramatic.

Will and Andy Cooper sat the porch while John Q crossed the meadow in the wagon.

"We thought shore ya was rustlers an' claim jumpers when we saw the smoke," Will said looking off towards the other two men.

"Now, ya know what happens in this country if someone 'bandons a place. It's open fer the first ta come 'long n' claim it!"

"You've some a the right 'bout thet, cept fer we din't abandon nuthin' an' ya know it. Ya seen our stock, food left in the house, all clean n' tight – ya know's no one is gonna jes up an' leave it thet way."

"We fig'red injuns, mebbe." It sounded weak even to Cooper's ears.

Will considered. "They been 'round. We get 'long with 'em. We done smoked peaceful with them chiefs."

"With injuns? Ya kin never trust 'em. Likely come back ta take yore hair soon's or late."

"Waal, be thet as it may, this place's is our'n."

Cooper looked around. "Tidy. Y'all done good. I been lookin' fer a place jes like this'n fer muh fam'ly ta come ta."

"Whar from?"

"Down Texas way. Ma n' pa, some brothers n' sisters jes been waitin' on me ta fig're whar ta git."

"Y'all Hashknife boys?"

"We trailed up here with 'em so I s'pose so. They kinder let us roam the range an' they pay found."

"From what I heerd, y'all ain't over-particular 'bout what ya find, neither. Muh pa had him a place up by Wilford an' been havin' some what ya might call diff'culties." Will looked evenly at Cooper.

"Boy, some places ya better be slappin' leather when ya said it. But yore right - Aztec been throwin' a wide loop. So thet cantankrous ol' coot be yer pa? I heerd he pulled stakes a while's back headin' ta ol' Mexico...."

"Thet's right. With you boys movin' in an' hoggin' the range even thar in Wilford it was getting' more'n a body could take without some significant hurtin'."

"I'll give ya a hunch it ain't gonna git much better, neither. Boys're movin' inter thet lil valley. Homes empty now'n all. More critters comin' from Texas on the railroad too. Gonna drop 'em all over the Aztec range," Cooper said.

189

"They'll overgraze if they're not careful. Ya best pass 'long thet muh sister is still up thar, married ta an ol' boy name a Richardson, an' we'll not take kindly ta them bein' fooled with."

Cooper looked serious. "I'll keep it ta mind. But I ain't in charge an' some a them boys kin be a trifle rough."

John Q stepped up on the porch with his Winchester in hand. "Waal, don't this look friendly! Y'all goin' in partners on the ranch, Will?" He smiled.

Cooper laughed. "I 'spect yore brother was about some few seconds from throwin' a gun or two on me, when them other boys started in huggin' an' kissin' an' what-not."

John Q looked at Edge and Cass still in close conversation and shook his head. "The Lord's wonders never cease!"

◆

"What in hell ever come a pa, Edge?"

"Soldier boys come 'long in a buckboard an' ended up shootin' 'im. Drug 'im off a ways. I was under our wagon while they took a few things an' drove off. They din't see me or they woulda finished me sho'nuff. I grabbed up pa's gun from by the fire whar I guess they din't see it an' went ta find 'im. He was dead so I just crawled up nexta 'im. Shot a few times when a wolf come snuffin' aroun'. Next thing I know Will's pa found me an' they took me in. Couldn't talk fer a while. When I could I din't know how ta find y'all. An' here I be.

"How come the soldiers ta kill pa?"

"No idear. Ta rob us, I guess. Upshot was, pa was plannin' on robbin' *them* 'til he saw they was soldiers."

Cass sighed. "Sounds like pa. Hell's bells, boy! It been more'n 20 years since I saw ya. Now yer all grown an' a real man!"

"What happened ta Able an' Broc an' Dirk? Where they at these days?"

"Able n' Broc went off ta fight the Yankees an' never come home. I reckon they got kil't

191

somewhar 'long the line, but never did hear nothin'. Dirk was with me in Texas 'til a few years back. We'd just started a drive ta find a place a our own an' his horse took a fall. Hit his head just wrong. He's buried over in the panhandle."

"Rough luck. Sorry ta hear it. Didya get a spread somewhere's? How'd ya come ta be here?"

"Injuns run off our stock after killin' the cook an' jes left me be. Hashknife was trailin' cows up here fer the Aztec an' needed hands. I worked fer 'em back in Texas, so I hitched up ag'in.

"Thet thar Cooper is a low-down sneak an' a four-flusher. Two a him won't make half a cowboy an' I jes been treadin' water waitin' ta git shet a him. He talked me inter comin' up here ta jump this place with 'im but any fool could see someone was gonna be comin' back fer the claim. Too much work been done ta jes up an' leave it."

"Ya got thet right, brother. Will was about one held breath away from throwin' guns. An' take it from me, thet boy ain't nothin' nobody wants no part of. I ain't no slouch spittin' lead, but thet boy

192

kin do with both a his Colts what I kin do with jes one. Hell on wheels ain't in it."

Cass was thoughtful. "Yep, he's the look. I've seen some real an' true bad men in Texas an' they all got thet same look. Both a ya do. Thet's probly why Cooper backed his heels so quick. He's more yella than true-blue."

◆

Will walked back to the wagon with John Q to help bring in supplies.

"Mary, you kin come on 'long now. We're home," John Q said.

"What aboot thet man sittin' up thar? He a-comin' ta supper?" she asked good-naturedly.

"I 'spect we'll have an extry couple a hands ta feed, darlin'." He helped her down.

"Hey, Will," he started, once she was out of earshot. "What's his story anyhow?"

"He was squattin' hopin' nobody would come back 'long."

"Kinder figured. An' ya convinced him otherwise?"

"I din't have no chance. Edge an' thet other cowboy figured out they was brothers somehow an' everythin' turned peaceful of a sudden. But listen here...I got me an idear we might could use this ta advantage."

John Q looked at them again. "What're the odds a thet! Out here in the high boondocks...heck, I din't even know he had a brother 'cept fer us.

"So what's yer big hunch? Tell it!"

Will told it.

◆

Supper finished, the men lounged in the cool twilight, Cooper and Cass smoking.

John Q knew he had to be delicate about their idea to get Cooper to buy their ranch. "So ya say ya got a big fam'ly back ta Texas, huh?"

"Shore do. Fig're on bringin' 'em out here if I kin ever find us a place."

"An' ya cottoned ta what we done here?"

"Yep. Like I said before – tidy. Y'all don't seem ta have ta worry 'bout the sheep men outa the south, yet. Country 'round like it is an' mebbe ya won't never hafta. But I figure me n' Bellows kin find us sumthin' close ta this. It's a big country."

"Thet it is. We looked this here over 'fore we homesteaded it an' it's the best around, not a doubt of it."

Cooper rolled another cigarette.

"Lemme ask y'all a question. Ya brung in supplies but not near 'nuff ta see ya through the winter. What's yore plan?"

Will laughed. "What, ya think we might pull out ag'in for ya ta come waltzin' back in?" This was working better than they planned.

"Naw, now hear me out. What would ya say ta mebbe we buy y'all out? Cash money on the barrel head."

195

Cass spoke up then. "Hold a minute or two, thar, Andy. Ya know I been hankerin' ta move on further west fer a while. Now thet I found muh brother, I been thinkin' on it even more." He looked at Edge who nodded.

"Fact is, I got some money saved from sellin' our farm thet's rightfully half Edge's now. We talked some 'bout mebbe partnerin' up."

John Q and Will were taken aback. "Thet right, Edge?" John Q asked and everyone waited for a reply.

It was some time in coming. When he spoke it was a low rumble tinged with emotion. "Truth is, boys, I never really wanted ta go ta Mexico. With ma n' pa already down thar, I woulda gone with y'all, but now thet Cass is here, it makes things diff'rent. Not thet I ain't grateful fer ever'thin' y'all ever done fer me. But sometimes a man's gotta take a new path. Y'all are kin, but Cass's muh blood-kin. I fig're we got some time ta make up."

Too many things were happening too fast for Will - he and Edge were close. He couldn't imagine the difference it would be not having his

196

silent older brother around. A pit formed where his stomach normally sat. It was the same feeling he'd had when he learned Domer was gone without a proper goodbye. He'd been able to set that aside since she was out of sight, but this was staring him in the face. Edge was looking at him but Will found he couldn't speak. He got to his feet and walked out to the corrals.

The almost-full moon was peeking over the mountain tops to the east when Edge joined him.

"Sorry ta spring thet on ya, Will. Yer folks saved muh life, but muh hardest leave-takin' is you."

"Thar yer folks too," Will said softly.

"I know it."

"I never knew ya din't wanna go ta Mexico. I guess I been so caught up in the idear a seein' Domer ag'in this here jes snuck up on me."

"I wasn't gonna say nuthin'. But now thet Cass is here...I jes fig'red mebbe it was time ta go a new way. Try sumthin' else out. If it don't work I kin always ketch up with y'all down thar."

197

"Brother, I got a feelin' thet ain't gonna happen."

Edge sighed. "We never kin tell, Will. The Lord don't promise us no tomorrows. We'll jes hafta wait an' see."

"A man's gotta go his way. I jes allays fig'red you'd be thar on *my* way. I lean on ya," Will said candidly.

"Tell ya sumthin', li'l brother - ya ever need me, all ya got ta do is holler - no matter whar I'm at I'll come runnin'."

Will knew it was the truth, but didn't know the promise would take 25 years to fulfill.

The two men discussed the moon high into the night sky. Nothing changed. Respect only obtained from long and close association manifest on both sides.

The knowledge of fast-approaching last-partings thickened the darkness.

◆

Andrew Blevins, aka Andy Cooper bought the Canyon Creek Ranch for $200 cash with one proviso: that the Adams boys never reveal he had paid them any money for it. His reputation as a "bad" man would stay intact until he ultimately crossed the wrong folks once too often and was found lacking.

He did send for his family who then became entangled and mostly exterminated in the Pleasant Valley War. The Blevins outfit rustled and stole and generally desperadoed their way to infamy. But that sad and sordid chapter of the west has been well-chronicled elsewhere, guilt enough to pass around on all sides.

Our Bellows brothers now ride out of our story here only to resurface in the pages of others – western immortality granted them in Nevada, where the CE Ranch and brand they were to create shared a long fence line and many adventures with the giant Ponderosa spread of legend and fame.

Edge would never see Will or many of his adopted family again, though he thought often and fondly of them all.

As for John Q and Will, only a few short months later, they gathered their wits, cattle and horses and pointed them all towards the land of *mañana*, where a pretty girl, a new life and the inevitability of a changing world all awaited to take up a hand at their table.

◆

Part IV

Mexico

Colonia Díaz – April, 1887

Domer Jones threw the wash-water out into the back yard, momentarily settling the dust. The Davis's seven month-old baby girl, Ashley, was settled comfortably in the crib which her father Brady had made for her, on her back, trying to eat her rattle. She was a delightful baby, with a wide smile and wildly gesticulating arms whenever she'd see Domer, her favorite person beside her mother, Shelter.

Brady was off talking to some newly arrived people to Díaz, while Shelter was helping at the Johnson house with clothes mending. Only heaven knew what either set of twins was into and James was out tending some stock for Orson

Richin, one of the largest cattlemen in the area. Domer had the house to herself.

The morning was rather ordinary - the late spring sun already warming the parched land under a cloudless sky. The rainy season had yet a few months to begin. There were only sporadic showers mixed with a few downpours from September until June. Their average rainfall was almost twelve inches, but nine of that came in the three summer months.

Díaz was finally taking shape since the land had been purchased from Ignacio del Campo the previous October – 7,000 acres in all, just a few short miles north of La Ascención, hard by the life-giving Casas Grandes river.

Mud construction with dirt floors and roofs was the order of the day as no other building materials were readily available. Brady Davis, as well as many of the other men, had become proficient adobe makers by necessity, taught the ancient art masterfully practiced by their native Mexican neighbors.

Picking Ashley from her crib, she walked out to sit in one of the hand-made rockers on their front stoop. Ashley was a little fussy today, but enjoyed rocking and it was pleasant under the shady porch. Domer watched the sparse activity along the street.

A lone horseman down near 1st street rode slowly towards her, still far enough away Domer could not make out who it was. She became slightly frustrated with herself because there was something very familiar about that rider. Recognition tickled at her mind.

◆

John Q, Mary and Will had arrived at the large community pasture northwest of the town with their cattle and remuda about the time Domer was finishing cleaning up the breakfast mess.

A joyous reunion with JJ, who was at the pasture tending some of his own cattle as well as those belonging to others, was followed by another a short time later with his mother, Mary at their spanking-new little house near the river.

Of course, one of the first things both JJ and Mary wanted to know about was Edge.

"He's doin' fine, ma. It's jes thet we happened to run inter his older bother tryin' ta squat on our ranch, an' after thet Edge, he decided ta go on 'long with 'im an' try ta start a ranch a their own." Will didn't really know how to explain it any better to his mother.

"Tryin' ta steal yer ranch thar at Canyon Crick?" JJ shook his head. "So Edge's brother was the outlaw type?

"Naw. Not really. The feller he was with, name a Cooper, he fancied hisself a bad hombre. But Cass, thet's Edge's brother, he was jes kinder thar with 'im. When he found out it was our'n, he backed off purty quick. Was more Coopers idear.

"Ma, ya could tell them two was jes 'like. Favored each other."

"Well," she sighed, "We always knew he might have kinfolk somewhar's. I do miss thet boy, though."

"He said ta give ya a big 'ol smackeroo," Will grinned.

Pleasantries were exchanged with other siblings - it was a companionable reunion for the Adams family that day, good spirits filling all in attendance.

◆

"Pa, whar's Domer at?" He was almost afraid to hear the answer. While on the trail south he'd fretted over the possibility she'd already gotten married or, worse, didn't want to see him.

His father laughed. "Ya been here, what, alla two minutes?" Will reddened with a blush he wished he could hide.

"Aw, now don't git all bent outa shape. She's jes over ta the Davis house corner a Dublan street an' 10th. Purtiest ya ever saw. The 'dobe house, thet is." He winked at John Q and they both burst into laughter.

"Now ya leave Will be, JJ. An' you too, John Q. Ya both oughta be ashamed a yerselves." Mary took a scolding tone, but she also had a wry set to her face that belied her words. She was having a hard time not laughing as well.

"Thanks a heap, alla ya."

Will assumed an appropriate huff, but even he had to smile as he got on his horse. How could he not? His mother would have said something if Domer was already married and besides, if she was still living with the Davis family that was a good sign.

His stomach a-flutter, but head in the clouds, if there had been any that is, Will made his way north to 1st street and turned left until he came to Dublan street, just one west of Main. Then he turned back north, trying to keep his heels from digging into Blue's sides.

◆

The horse was different, but there was no mistaking the way Will sat a saddle even from fifth all the way to where she sat at tenth. Domer's breath caught in her suddenly tight throat. A hand went to her mussed hair and she blanched. She hurried inside carrying the sleeping Ashley and laid her in the crib gently.

The moment she was free she rushed to make herself presentable. *Hurry up! He'll be here any moment!*

◆

Thet's not quite the reception I was hopin' fer.

Will had thought of all kinds of ways Domer might react, but running away wasn't on the list.

I know she saw me ridin' up. Why would she run off thet way?

Mebbe she don't wanna see ya, Will.

Naw. I can't believe thet!

She never even wrote ya a letter. Took off without sayin' goodbye. Not a note or a word left.

207

Mebbe she din't know it was me. It's been more'n a year.

Yer a fool if ya git down offa this horse an' go knockin' on thet door. A pure-d fool.

Aw, hush up! I gotta find out fer sure.

His conversation with himself over, he dismounted and looked around. He was alone, but felt like everyone in the town was watching him and laughing, knowing what he was there for. He waited a while longer.

Mebbe she'll come back out...

◆

What in ternation is takin' him so long? Was thet boots at the door?

Domer had hastily thrown herself together and was now waiting for a knock...

But none came. And then none came again.

This is jes dumb! Is he waitin' on me ta come runnin'?

But what if he left? Mebbe he saw me come in an' fig'red I din't wanna see him? Oh no. Thet's gotta be it.

She jumped out of the chair and ran to the front door, snatching it open just as Will raised his hand to knock.

"Will Adams what's yer idear a makin' me wait an' fret ya wasn't comin' after all?" Domer exclaimed more sharply than she meant to.

Will's face turned from surprise to cloudy. "Waal, wha'd'ya mean by runnin' off so's I had ta come git ya? An' wha'd'ya mean me makin' *you* wait?"

A coy smile played across her lips. "I had ta fix my hair. Ya din't gimme no warnin'. All of a sudden there ya was down the street. I 'bout fainted. 'Sides, the way I fig're it yer 'bout a year late."

Will relented immediately, missing her joke. "We jes got here not an hour since. After muh ma's place, this's the first place I come ta visit."

Domer's toe peeked from underneath the hem of her dress. Head bowed, she drew a lazy circle in the hard-packed dirt floor. She looked up at him demurely. "I'm glad ya come. I been waitin' on ya," she spoke low and sweet. Her soft answer calmed the troubled beast.

Words never were uttered more welcome to a suitor's ears. His mood changed in an instant - he swept her into his arms. They held each other with an urgent embrace that was far too long in arriving. An electric feeling, magnified by time apart, passed between them such as only soul-mates are blessed to understand.

They kissed and her tears spilled down his cheeks. They were home.

We'll draw the curtain now for a little while on that reunion – the sickly-sweet things uttered might make us, at this remove, a little condescending in our smugness. But let which of us who hasn't made of them self a fool for love, and many times over, snicker the first. We'll give them their privacy.

◆

"So why'd ya up an' leave without even a whisper of a goodbye?"

They sat close to each other on the porch, Ashley back in Domer's arms, playing with Will's hat and dropping it every few seconds, delighted with herself for doing so and getting it back so easily.

"Ya'd run off ta the mountains ta play cowboy without me an' I fig'red ya weren't comin' back fer a-while. I wrote ya two letters, but they jes din't say how I really felt an' then I wondered if'n mebbe ya was jes tryin' ta let me down easy. I worried the whole time we was comin' down here an' I been worried the whole time we been here thet mebbe I was never gonna see ya ag'in. An' then there ya was, tall in the saddle, big as life an' all my worryin' gone."

Will shook his head. "I kinder thought ya might have already got married by the time I showed up. Once we fig'red on leavin' ta come

211

down here, it didn't seem like we could git outa the country fast enough fer me. Yer even purtier than ya were an' thet's sayin' sumthin'."

She laughed and the sound thrilled him. "I'm a mess! We've only moved in here a few months back an' I haven't had a chance ta make any nice clothes or git myself fixed up anythin' close ta purty." Nevertheless, she secretly enjoyed the fact that Will liked her looks.

"Ya don't need any fixin' up. Look here, Domer, I done asked yer pa back ta Arizona if'n I could marry ya when I got here an' he give me permission. Ma Bonnie had tears in her eyes, so I told 'em if ya said yes I'd bring ya back up there so's they could see ya married off proper. I still got ta ask Brady fer yer hand 'cause he's responsible fer ya now, but I fig're I kin talk ta him later. I'm asking ya now: Domer, will ya marry me? I know we kin make a good life together if you'll have me."

She and Ashley both smiled at him. "Looks like yer finally gonna throw thet loop on one wife, anyway. Yes, Will Adams, I will marry ya gladly."

"I ain't never gonna need another! Guess I'll git rid a muh rope now thet ya said yes," he teased her.

Ashley's arms and legs thrashed and she got such a big smile on her chubby-cheeked face that her eyes almost shut.

"Lookit thet smile, Domer - I'd say she agrees with the weddin' plans. Kid, ya better stop throwin' muh good hat on the ground!" He picked it up again and engulfed Ashley's head with it.

"I din't know ya had more'n one hat."

He laughed. "I don't, but don't tell her thet!"

1890-1902

Seasons came and went and passed into years.

It turned out Will and Domer did very well at making little boys.

William Adams, Jr. was born in 1889, followed by seven more children spread over twelve years. The fourth child, one of only two girls out of the final total of eleven, was named for her mother, Domer, but went by her middle name Edith.

Díazites planted fruit trees and fast-growing elms and cottonwoods. Deep, hand-dug canals tamed and utilized the river for irrigation. Shade lengthened and more streets appeared; a grist mill, a blacksmith and a store or two.

More people arrived, some born, others by wagon, horse or foot. Houses of wood and brick were built with materials freighted from Deming, New Mexico, 90 miles to the north. Floors of dirt were replaced and window openings gained glass and sprouted curtains.

Untold man and woman hours turned the inhospitable desert landscape into a shady, latter-day Eden.

Herds grew in size and quality. Young boys became delinquent at school in favor of the cowboy profession, distressing their prim and proper teachers.

Over it all smiled a munificent sun, giving life and killing germ. A land bathed in such 340 days in a year can't help but have health promoted and dispositions improved.

Shining moments multiplied - peace and prosperity were abundantly scattered in the area of Díaz. Those were indeed wonderful salad days in multitudinous other fashions unnamed.

But not everything was sweetness and light. As in all of life, opposition sharpens the taste of good, and for such a blessed community there seemed to be an equal number of trials.

Some came from less-industrious native neighbors, jealous of the apparent steady success and the imagined riches which came with it.

Some came from officially sanctioned graft – a built-in, permanent way of life in their adopted country from time immemorial. The Customs House provided ample opposition to the newly arrived, often from the very first. Will and John Q found this out to their chagrin the day after they came to Díaz, when officials appeared to systematically catalog each of their meager belongings, charging them $17.50 tax on their used wagon alone.

Some came from the increasingly turbulent times in which they lived – unrest spreading throughout the world and coming to awful fruition in the first two decades of the 20th century. From Singapore to San Francisco, from Saint Petersburg to Sydney, new political "isms" were sweeping forth and Mexico was not immune. Communist organizers stirred anger into the hearts of mine workers against their Capitalist "oppressors". More often than not the developers of these mines included moneyed and privileged *Norteamericanos* – strong sentiments bubbled on slow boil in these cauldrons of labor.

Some guilt by association rubbed off onto each of the colonies in Mexico since they too were from the United States. Unspoken resentments festered against newcomers.

Will wore his guns constantly. Increasingly, he became known among both the good and evil elements with a reputation for not only being very fast with his guns, but also for never hesitating to use them when needed. He obtained a nickname for which he didn't care - *"Dos-Pistolas"* was what the *bandidos* called him. It stuck whether he wanted it or not. Two-Gun.

Cinco de Mayo, 1902

The funeral was one of the largest Díaz had seen to that point. "Grandpa" Adams, as JJ had become known, was a popular figure among both the colonists and indigenous Mexican population.

217

His even-handedness, humor and jovial nature won him the respect of all he came in contact with. And since Mary frequently midwifed for the locals as well as colonists, JJ received additional adulation from her reflection.

His death threw a cloud over the area. He had been there from the first when, landless, the colonists had camped in tents by the river next to La Ascención, under an order of imminent expulsion by the Governor of Chihuahua, only rescinded at the last minute by Porfirio Díaz himself. It led, once they finally did succeed in purchasing land, to the naming their new colony in honor of the Mexican president who had protected them.

That was back when the locals had looked with much fear and suspicion on their forced new neighbors from the *Estados Unidos*. However, from their peaceful attitude, they soon won over the hearts of the people of La Ascención and the surrounding area and no one helped more in this than JJ. He picked up the language quickly, having the gift of a nimble brain and tongue – his ever-present, ready smile and honest mannerisms all combined to gain him friends everywhere he went.

He aged well. The "Grandpa" appellation came as he grew into the patriarch figure for Díaz, akin to Abraham of antiquity, sought out for and pronouncing blessings upon his family and friends.

His death, though natural, was a blow. However, his funeral celebrated his life, as Mormon funerals sometimes have a unique way of doing, concentrating on his family and their hope of continued familial associations in the hereafter. Many a tear was shed that day as might well be imagined - but their belief in bright tomorrows was reaffirmed.

Hans Mickelson created the marker out of sandstone with a fitting representation of JJ's momentous life.

Casas Grandes – May 4, 1905

Events in Mexico were fast combining and then rearranging themselves in different ways to become increasingly successful at rendering chaos from order.

Although the colonists began to sense the undercurrents, far-flung, seemingly insignificant happenings would coalesce to result in significant changes to their lives.

These events were rushing along towards a conclusion few could guess at and fewer would have desired. One link in that long chain was the grand "hunting" expedition of W.C. Greene.

A free-wheeling capitalist of the first order, Greene was loosed upon sleepy northern Mexico about when the centuries changed. By the time his life had run its mercurial course a few years later, he had created, almost single-handedly, the enormous gold, silver and copper mining enterprise at Cananea in the Mexican state of Sonora and had, at one time or another, controlled a large part of the northern portion of that state, as well as parts of Chihuahua. He built railroads, towns and ranches – his RO ranch spanned the border between Sonora and Arizona. The RO alone was a fourth again larger than Rhode Island or about the same size as Delaware.

President Porfirio Díaz foresaw that wealthy Americans could bring jobs and much-needed currency to the resource-rich, but undeveloped, backward and largely unsettled areas of northern Mexico. He believed it good for his country's future and encouraged the Americans to invest heavily in the area. He authorized huge land and mineral concessions to entice that investment. It was one of the policies that eventually led to the revolution and his being toppled from power in 1911.

At the epicenter of this massive effort was Greene, who made and spent several fortunes along the way. He gave himself the title of "Colonel" and was a first-name contemporary of such grandiose and colorful characters as E.H. Harriman, Epes Randolph, William Rockefeller

221

and James Stillman. He had a well-earned reputation for entertaining his friends and business associates lavishly.

Ammon Tenney, son of Woodruff, Arizona founder Nathan, was hired to guide the hunting expedition and given *carte blanche*. He recruited more than a dozen of the best outdoors-men he knew - Will Adams topped the list.

The outfitters had instructions to round up and hold deer, elk and bears, so that the industrialists, politicos, and garden variety American millionaire investors, most of whom knew nothing or next to it about real hunting, might have something to remember.

Among the notable invitees who were quite capable in the out-of-doors in their own right were Tom Powers, the famous one-eyed barman of El Paso, and Burton Mossman, Captain of the Arizona Rangers and honcho of the aforementioned Aztec ranch. Sheriff Pat Garrett, who had achieved wide-spread fame by killing the notorious and admired bandit, Billy the Kid, was along too.

Two of the guides awaited the millionaires set to arrive in Casas Grandes from El Paso by a private train belonging to Greene.

Both Ammon and Will were by that time fairly jaundiced against the whole enterprise as might be expected of two capable and practical men. The balance of the Mormon guides were 85 miles further into the wilderness where an elaborate base camp had appeared out of thin air.

The locals watched the proceedings with a little sardonic humor and more than a little anger and resentment at the gaudy intrusion and apparent profligate waste.

Pathetic gringos, they thought almost to a person. *How do people so inept and stupid have so much money?*

Two worlds further apart could scarcely be imagined. And yet, there they were, suddenly thrust into close contact. Both groups were suspicious, ignorant and contemptuous, but each would have been equally surprised to learn their opposite's attitudes were identical.

◆

"When're the big-wigs s'posed ta show up?" Will asked, using his bandana to swat away the obnoxious biting flies. They sat in the shade, one eye watching for the train and the other making sure nobody "appropriated" any of their expensive preparations.

"They don't have a schedule they let me in on, Will. They'll be here when they get here, I guess. All's I know is it was supposed to be today sometime or other."

"I'll bet it's other, then. I can't believe I let ya talk me inter this. Nursemaid'n a bunch a sissies from back east. Roundin' up deer! Roundin' up b'ars! Jees Louise, Ammon. I've a good mind ta round me up some few millionaires an' drive 'em ta meet them b'ars personal."

"Well, just you remember they all got more money than Solomon, even if they might be a little shy on western know-how. That's where we come in and you better show some manners when they get here. The Colonel is paying you enough to keep your trap shut. And you know he's no pilgrim."

"Yep. But have ya felt the mood 'round here? *These* folks ain't gettin' paid none an' I got a feelin' they might could show some displeasure. We hired on as body guards *tambien, jefe*?"

"What do you think those guns you're always wearing are for, anyhow?" Ammon smirked at Will.

Will sniffed. "Huh. Not much I ain't shootin' locals in favor a wimps thet got more dollars than sense."

"Let's hope it doesn't come to that. I do know what you mean, though. I've seen quite a few hard looks thrown our way. Lucky thing they know 'bout 'ol mister Two-Gun. I doubt we'll have any trouble."

"I shore wonder how thet name got a start. I'm not partial ta it. Jes an invite fer any would-be or wanna-be ta come outa the woodwork lookin' ta make a bad-man rep."

"Well, boo-hoo. I'm all broken up inside. If they only knew what a tin-horn you really are and how those guns're just for show, that old lady over there would probably take you on."

Will laughed. "Alrighty then le's not tell 'er, huh?"

"Keep complaining and maybe I will."

"I'll hush. She looks purty tough."

Fortunately, just at that moment the welcome sound of a train whistle was heard. They could make out a smoke trail billowing from the stack, following lazily along in the still air.

"How many cars you see, Will?" Ammon knew his friends eyesight was much keener than his own.

"I kin make out three fer sure 'sides the coal car an' a caboose. Thet thar is the way ta cover some country in style. Think they got any a thet caviar in thar? Allays wanted ta try out some a thet."

"I wouldn't be surprised. Ask the Colonel for some. They probably hired us Mormons 'cause they knew we wouldn't drink up all their

226

champagne and smoke their Cuban stogies," he laughed.

Will laughed too. "No doubt."

◆

The rest of "The Great Hunt" was relatively uneventful and the tenderfeet weren't quite as tender as Will had worried. Even though some of them were pampered more than seemed right, what with such luxuries as an in-camp barber and masseuse, on balance they required less baby-sitting than expected.

One event during the hunt had the millionaires talking for years afterward and is worth relating for our story.

These men of the east, financiers and tycoons of business with mighty political clout, equally at home on Wall Street or in Washingtonian chambers, were in awe of Pat Garrett there in the wilds of Mexico.

He was constantly peppered with questions about Billy the Kid and how Garrett had tracked him down and killed him at Fort Sumner.

Pat, as was true of many western men of the time, didn't go in for a lot of braggadocio or lurid details, preferring instead to let deeds do their own talking. This was unheard of where these powerful men came from - hustle and self-promotion were a way of life. So the millionaires persisted.

One evening, after a contented supper of fresh venison and turkey was followed by the equally contented puffing of expensive cigars and imbibing of select drink, the party lounged and returned to its favorite pastime - pestering Pat Garrett for more stories of the romantic and mysterious west.

In truth, Garrett didn't mind so much. But it wouldn't do to let on. He hemmed. He hawed. He hesitated and squirmed. He understood well the performer's art of timing, allowing himself to be coaxed *just* enough without it getting tiresome.

One of the company, who was himself an abominable shot, asked Pat who was the best gunman he had ever seen. The camp went quiet. The men listened. It was a worthy question asked of the exact right person. There were several good shooters in that very ring.

Pat contemplated. He scrunched his eyes. He looked this way and that. They awaited his portentous answer with smoky breath.

"Waal, let me think on that a few minutes," he drawled. "I've seen more'n a few men who've been really good with a gun. And then I've seen a few more. But one, more'n any other to my way of thinking, stands out above all the rest." The tease was wearing.

"Aw, come on, Pat. Just tell us and be done with it!" A chorus of agreement.

"He's right here in camp. This very now."

Silence. Furtive looks around.

"And he's.......me!"

Colonel Greene burst out laughing as did the rest of the men.

Garrett appeared suitably affronted by this disrespect and puffed his chest.

"So you don't think I'm serious, do you gentlemen? I'll tell you what – I'll give you odds I can out-shoot any man here. I've a hundred dollars says none of you can beat me."

Now these were men who needed a hundred dollars like their wives needed another diamond, but competitive spirit had driven each to the worldly heights they had achieved and it didn't desert them now. Immediate takers were on their feet on every side.

The guides watched - some cut their eyes in Will's direction who merely waited, seemingly with faint interest. Ammon was considering him with an amused expression.

"You want to make a hundred dollars?" he asked quietly.

Will glanced at him and then back to the group of jostling men.

"Alright, here is what we're going to do. We'll put five cans on each side of that tree. Then, whoever wants to try for the hundred can take out their pistol and shoot the cans as fast as they can. I'll do the same and whoever shoots his five cans first wins. Any questions?"

"What about a rifle?"

"You can shoot with a rifle if you want."

"But that doesn't seem hardly right, Pat. You're going to only use your pistol? And only with five shots in it?" Greene was known for his sense of fair play.

"Five is all I'll need. There's only five cans, correct?"

More laughter.

"Ok, it's your funeral. Who's first?"

Several stepped up. The contest was on. Time after time, man after man was turned away by the unerring accuracy of Pat's gun. Pistol or rifle, no one even came close.

Greene and all gathered were genuinely impressed. "Kings X! You proved your point. That's some pretty fancy shooting, alright. No wonder you got the Kid."

"Billy might have beaten me," Garrett said, almost to himself.

"Well? Is that all? Nobody else wants to try?" he asked, confident he had shut them all up.

Ammon Tenney spoke up quietly. "Colonel, is the contest only open to you all or can some of us cowboys take part?"

Everyone looked at the forgotten group of their guides. Then they looked at Greene who was looking at Garrett. Garrett laughed. "Hell yes you can get in on this. But the prize for y'all is fifty. Might somebody get lucky," he hedged.

"Oh come now, Pat! Any one of them beats you he'll have earned his hundred. I'll put it up myself!" Greene said with a flourish. The rest of the men laughed, beaten to the punch by Greene once again. "Who wants to try?"

The group of Mormons looked around at each other, then at Will. He stepped forward.

"I guess I'll give 'er a whirl."

The men cheered his gumption. The cans were reset. Garrett reloaded his gun. Will eased his in their holsters.

"You gonna need 'em both?" Garrett asked with a smile.

"Never kin tell." Will smiled right back.

Poor cowboy. Everybody wants to beat the legend, they all thought. *Still...he looks pretty confident.*

Greene stood between and behind Will and Pat. "I'm gonna throw this pine cone in front of you – when it hits the ground commence to shooting! We'll all be the judges. You both ready?"

They each nodded.

"Here she goes!" He tossed the cone high into the air.

Will concentrated as he'd taught himself to do countless times in the past. All the years of practice distilled into these few moments. He would "feel" rather than aim each bullet to its target. He suddenly had a vision of Porter Rockwell shooting similar cans those many years before. All of this passed through his mind in less than the time it took for the cone to reach the ground.

It finally did and seven cans disappeared. Five of them had been on Will's side of the tree.

Garrett stopped firing, dumbfounded and brought up short by his peripheral sight of cans no longer standing. Except for his own.

Calmly, Will de-cocked his left gun, the hammer subconsciously pulled back with the right – but the sixth shot wasn't necessary.

Shocked silence ruled for a few breaths.

Then pandemonium broke loose. Men of high station and low were exclaiming and shaking hands. Pat Garrett considered Will with another smile – this one a little admiring.

"Nice shooting, cowboy," was all he said, nodding.

Will smiled too. He ejected and pocketed the still warm empty brass and reloaded his guns.

He never did collect the money, though.

Cananea Consolidated Copper Company
Sonora – June 1, 1906

Another link in that chain of destiny leading to the revolution – some would say the real beginning of the revolution - happened at Cananea, Colonel Greene's colossal copper mine in Sonora.

For years the Four C's, as the mine was known, had paid its Mexican mine workers three *pesos* for a ten hour workday. This was several times what they could make working on a ranch or at almost any other job available at that time. As a result, the mine was constantly inundated with Mexican locals seeking a high-paying position. According to President Porfirio Díaz, who had encouraged American investment, the extremely high wages offered by Greene were disrupting the Mexican economy. He ordered those wages lowered at Cananea.

It was another of his mistakes.

Greene also had the ticklish proposition of trying to lure knowledgeable American miners to come work at Cananea, and, as at all other times of free-market labor, he had to pay for the mining experience needed to get at the copper the resistant earth held. Hence, wages paid to the Americans were more than double what was paid to the Mexicans, while at the same time on a par with or a little higher than what they could earn in the states.

Greene was a business man who understood he had to pay for talent.

And he was a progressive thinker who knew all too well the value of his native labor force. It was why he ran afoul of Mexico City when he paid the locals too much. But they were, in general, less experienced, so the market dictated the wages of the Mexican and American workers be different.

Into the gap leaped the agitators, seizing on the disparity as evidence of racism. This played perfectly into their true endgame of organizing mine workers into unions – not just in Mexico, but also in the United States at several locations.

The Four C's and Greene, caught in the middle, were damned for paying too much and damned for paying too little.

A strike was called at Cananea. The simple demands were five *pesos* for an eight hour work day. Over 2,000 workers gathered in the streets of the company town. By most accounts they were peaceful and many were wearing their best clothes. Once activities had been stopped at the mining and combining operations, the strikers turned their attentions to the lumber yard where work still persisted.

Greene himself appeared among them to explain why he couldn't raise wages – his hands were tied by Mexico City. He was a popular figure among the workers and many returned to their company furnished homes after he asked them to. He also suggested a delegation be formed by the workers so they could present their grievances.

This wasn't good enough for the strike organizers who scoffed at his proposal and subsequently distributed an impassioned petition to those remaining, calling for rebellion and inciting violence. Temperature levels rose alarmingly. The increasingly unruly crowd marched to the lumber yard.

No one knows for certain what really happened that morning at the chained lumber yard gates, but when the smoke finally cleared, the yard had been burned to the ground, three Mexican workers had been shot and lay dead in the street along with the two American bosses of the yard, the Metcalf brothers, George and William.

The first blood of the Mexican revolution had been spilled.

Chihuahua and Sonora – 1910-1911

All across northern Mexico with a final push southwards to the capital, Francisco Madero's volunteer army won victory after victory against the *Federales* of Porfirio Díaz, eventually driving him to Europe, out of power and into exile, where he died a few years later.

One of Madero's most capable commanders was one Francisco Villa. Known for little more than banditry, terrorizing the wealthy land owners, the *hacendados*, in the decade preceding the revolution, Pancho Villa, more than anyone, would become hero to the common people - the *peónes*. Unlike almost every other revolutionary leader, notwithstanding that he would eventually become Governor of the State of Chihuahua, he had little pretension to power.

Ever after he was suspected by those actually in power precisely because of his popularity. Leaders throughout the revolutionary times judged Villa through the prism of their own ambitious natures and assumed he must be plotting against them. They weren't alone of mankind in making that same mistake.

Eventually, petty jealousies would become full-bore resentments and the hero would be assassinated in 1923.

Villa would also plan and execute one of the only raids into the United States proper in its history, crossing the border at Palomas and into Columbus, New Mexico, resulting in General "Black Jack" Pershing pursuing him and his men all over northern Mexico - one aide-de-camp being a young lieutenant by the name of Patton. World War I intervened with Pershing's army being recalled and Villa still at large having never been captured.

All of that was still far in a murky and uncertain future, though. Much more water would pass tranquilly down the Casas Grandes River by Díaz to finally empty into the *Laguna Guzmán* before any of those events would take place.

Richin's Ranch, South of Colonia Díaz – March 5, 1911

"I'm not sure what we'll find when we get there, Will. Remember, we need to be careful to remain neutral in these matters."

Brady Davis and Will Adams rode into the Orson Richin ranch to investigate reports of *bandidos* from La Ascención slaughtering Richin's beef cattle. Davis was armed only with a shotgun - Will had on his normal guns as he always did.

"I'm jes 'long ta hep ya. We let 'em rustle Orson's cows an' we might jes as well let 'em have alla ourn, too."

"Just you behave, you hear?" Davis said with a nervous smile. He knew Will wouldn't put up with any nonsense.

Yep, Bishop. Ya won't hear a peep outa me," Will replied a tad sarcastically.

A large group of men with horses were ahead in one of Richin's pastures. Several fires were lit and the distinctive smell of roasting meat pervaded the air. Davis recognized one of the leaders and mumbled curses almost to himself. Will looked over at him sharply – he'd seldom known Brady to use any language saltier than "durn".

They rode slowly towards the group. Will let himself go into that quiet place of intense concentration. The sixth cylinders were already loaded in both his Colts.

"Ah, el señor Davis, mi viejo amigo! ¿Has venido a celebrás con nosotros? ¿Y quién es este que viene con ustéd?" the man said, munching contentedly on meat still on the bone.

(Ah, Mr. Davis, my old friend! Have you come to celebrate with us? And who is this you bring with you?)

"Este es mi amigo, Will Adams. ¿Qué celebrás, el Sr. Pancho?"

(This is my friend, Will Adams. What are you celebrating, Mr. Pancho?)

This brought much merriment from the leader and his men who laughed hilariously.

"Ustéd ve, muchachos? Es por eso me gusta tanto! Sr. Pancho, él me llama! Nadie más que el Sr. Davis, el mormón, me llama así!" Everyone laughed again and it was infectious. Brady and Will did too.

(You see, boys? That is why I like him so much! Mr. Pancho, he calls me! No one but Mr. Davis, the great Mormon leader, calls me that!)

"Brady, sólo me llama Pancho, ¿Eh?" And then to his men: *"Esto me conocía antes de que tomara el nombre santo del padre de mi madre, Villa. Este hombre es un viejo amigo, un hombre bueno y verdadero."*

(Brady, you just call me Pancho, ok? This one knew me before I took the sainted name of my mother's father, Villa. This man is an old friend, a good man and true.)

His face was smiling and open. He seemed truly pleased to see Brady Davis again. Whatever tensions existed before had vanished as Villa spoke. Even so, a few of the men eyed the two armed visitors warily.

"Al suelo, por favor, los dos de ustéd y se unán a nosotros. Dime qué puedo hacer por mi viejo amigo."

(Get down, please, the both of you and join us. Tell me what I can do for my old friend.)

Brady and Will dismounted and they all sat on the ground together.

"¿Quieres agua? Sé que no va a beber mi tequila!" He laughed again.

(You want some water? I know you won't drink my tequila!)

"Un poco de agua estará bien, grácias, Pancho. Hoy he venido aquí para razonár con ustéd como los hombres. Verás, tenemos un pequeño problema. Este campo y el rancho pertenece a uno de los míos y el carne que están comiendo es de él. Sé que hablamos de cómo ustéd y sus hombres podría conseguir algunas vacas en el pasado, pero sería mejor para todos si ustéd me deja saber antes de que los matan

para que podemos hacer los arreglos necesarios."

(Some water would be fine, thank you, Pancho. I came here today to reason with you as men do. You see, we have a slight problem. This pasture and ranch belongs to one of my people and the beef you are eating is his. I know we talked about how you and your men could get some cows in the past, but it would be better for everyone if you let me know before you killed them so we can make arrangements.)

"Ah, sí. Sí hablamos de eso. Yo no sabía que era la tierra de su pueblo. Es tan cerca de La Ascensión que pensé que estaba en uno de los viejos ejidos. Mis hombres tenían hambre desde que tomamos Ascención, y entonces tomamos vacas también, ¿Entiendes?"

(Ah, yes. We did talk about that. I did not know this was your people's land. It is so close to La Ascención that I thought it was on one of the old *ejidos*. My men were hungry and since we took Ascención, we took their cows too, understand?)

245

"Perfectamente, jefe. Tenemos problemas con los bandidos de tomar ventaja de estos tiempos revolucionarios. Pero eso no es lo que tenemos aquí. Voy a explicar la situación al Sr. Richin, que trabaja esta tierra. Tal vez podemos decir que es una donación en especie. Sin embargo, ustéd sabe que somos neutrales, así es que por favór no dejes que sea conocida."

(Perfectly, boss. We have troubles with bandits taking advantage of these revolutionary times. But that is not what you are doing. I will explain the situation to Mr. Richin, who works this land. Maybe we can call it a donation in kind. However, you know we are neutral, so please don't let that be known.)

"Brady, tengo una idea. Deja que te pago para el carne de vaca y entonces ustéd puede pagar su hombre. De esta manera, los federales no pueden pretendér que nos ayudó, ¿eh?"

(Brady, I have an idea. Let me pay you for the beef and then you can pay your man. This way, the *Federales* cannot claim you helped us, eh?)

"Pancho, ustéd es un hombre de mucha comprensión," Davis said, smiling.

(Pancho, you are a man of much understanding.)

"Bueno! Según reiterada, entonces. Pero me puedes decír una cosa? Este amigo que traigas contigo. Admiro mucho la forma en que tiene una arma en cada cadera. Dime la verdad - es que un pistolero de los Estados Unidos que es para su protección?"

(Good! It is settled, then. But can you tell me one thing? This friend you bring with you. I much admire how he has a gun on each hip. Tell me the truth – is he a gunfighter from the United States you bring for protection?)

Brady laughed. *"Él es muy bueno con esas armas, es cierto, pero él es uno de nosotros en Díaz."*

(He's very good with those guns, it is true, but he's one of us there at Díaz.)

"Ah, esto es así. ¿Cómo es que lleva dos de ellos?"

(Ah, it is so. How come he wears two of them?)

Will had been listening, of course, and spoke up. *"Mi padre los compró para mí cuando yo era mucho más joven. Eso fue en los días en que más gente llevaba dos en lugar de uno solo. Nunca he conseguido salir de la costumbre."*

(My father bought them for me when I was much younger. That was back in the days when more people wore two instead of just one. I've never gotten out of the habit.)

"Eso tiene sentido. He oído hablar de ustéd. Algunos de los hombres que han hablado de que ustéd llama de "Dos-Pistolas". Ahora que te veo, que encaja. Creo que yo también te llamo el Señor Dos-Pistolas. Ustéd habla muy bien el español."

(That makes sense. I have heard of you. Some of the men who have talked about you called you Two-Gun. Now that I see you, it fits. I think I will also call you Mr. Two-Gun. You speak Spanish very well.)

Will didn't like the name but kept quiet about it. His guns were part of him – not something he showed off. *"Gracias, señor Villa. He vivido aquí unos veinte años."*

(Thank you, Mr Villa. I've lived here about twenty years.)

"Ustéd es un hombre a tener en cuenta, dicen. ¿Le importaría darnos una demostración de su habilidad?"

(You are a man to be reckoned with, they say. Would you care to give us a demonstration of your skill?)

Will hesitated, looking at Davis. It had been years since he had done any shooting competitions. But all that practice in his youth had ingrained muscle memory that didn't go away. Plus, there was that competition with Pat Garrett a few years back...

"No le gusta hacer alarde de sí mismo o de presumír, normalmente. Adelante Will. Dales un espectáculo como en los viejos tiempos!" Brady was egging him on now.

(He doesn't like to boast about himself or show off, normally. Go ahead Will. Give them a show like in the old days!)

Will grinned. He got up and went about forty feet away and placed two small rocks five feet apart. Then he walked back to Villa and Davis, double checking and preparing his guns by ejecting the sixth rounds from each.

"Dile a tus hombres a mirár. A ver si me acuerdo de cómo hacer esto. Sr. Villa, si vas a aplaudír tres veces, en el tercero, voy a ver si me pueden golpear una de esas rocas."

(Tell your men to watch. Let's see if I remember how to do this. Mr. Villa, if you'll clap three times, on the third one, I'll see if I can hit one of those rocks.)

The men had gathered around – shooting demonstrations were something they understood very well and respected.

Villa was smiling. *"¿Listo?"* He started clapping and counting in time. *"Uno, dos, Tr..."*

(Ready? One, Two, Thr...)

He hadn't finished saying three when Will pulled and cocked both of his Colts, firing nearly simultaneously.

The noise from the shots died away, leaving a total silence as Villa and his men alternately stared at where both rocks used to be and then back at Will, disbelievingly.

"¡Eso es imposible!" Villa screamed with a hearty laugh.

(That's impossible!)

At once his men were laughing too and patting Will on the back appreciatively. Many shook their sombreros with raised eyebrows, hands clapping and exclaiming. Some looked at his guns as if they might jump out of their holsters and do more tricks at any moment.

251

"Dios mío, eso era increíble! Increíble!" Villa proclaimed. *"Así que las historias son verdaderas, ¿Eh Brady? El Sr. Dos Pistolas."*

(My God, that was amazing! Amazing! So the stories are true, eh Brady? Mr. Two-Gun.)

Brady smiled. *"Te lo díje, viejo amigo. Algunos de nosotros gringos realmente podemos disparár!"*

(I told you, old friend. Some of us gringos can really shoot!)

Villa laughed again. *"Eso es cierto. Nunca he visto nada iguál."*

(That is true. I've never seen anything like it.)

They talked and sat around for a while longer. Soon though, Brady sensed it was time to go.

"Gracias de nuevo, mi viejo amigo. Ha sido bueno verte," he said, not mentioning the money for the beef.

(Thank you again, my old friend. It has been good to see you.)

"Para mí también. Voy a pasar la palabra que el pueblo de Díaz deben ser dejados solos," he said magnanimously with a flourish of his hand.

(For me too. I will pass the word that the people of Díaz should be left alone.)

"Y Brady! Aquí es un poco de dinero para esas vacas. No es mucho - no somos más que los pobres."

(And Brady! Here is a little money for those cows. Not so much – we are but poor people.)

"Es sufeciente, Pancho. Ahora, si nos disculpa? Tenemos que volvér a Díaz para que todos sepan lo que pasó aquí hoy y cómo está, como siempre, un hombre honorable!"

(It is sufficient, Pancho. Now if you'll excuse us? We need to get back to Díaz and let everyone know what happened here today and how you are, as always, an honorable man!)

"Ah, me vergüenza, Brady. Yo soy, como tú, sólo un hombre! Pero que Dios está con ustédes hasta que nos encontramos de nuevo."

253

(Ah, you shame me, Brady. I am, like you, just a man! But may God be with you both until we meet again.)

Davis smiled as he and Will shook Villa's hand. *"Y contigo, viejo amigo."*

(And with you, old friend.)

Villa and his men watched the two ride away, some still shaking their heads and discussing Will's shooting spectacle.

Colonia Díaz – July 1, 1912 – 4:52pm

The past week Domer had felt herself growing weaker. She could hardly raise up in bed to take the thin broth Mary tried to feed her.

"You must keep up your strength, dear," she would say when Domer refused. "For yourself an' the baby."

"Mother, I have a feelin' it's not gonna matter."

"That'll be quite enough of that talk. I've not lost a mother nor child yet. You aren't gonna be the first!" She hoped her bravado would mask her own deep misgivings.

Continually wringing out the dish towel she had placed on Domer's forehead, she tried to give her some measure of coolness against the late afternoon sun.

The room seemed dirty to Domer. If she could have got up from her bed she would have been on her hands and knees scrubbing every corner of their home. Funny how she felt the nesting urge strongly, but had no energy to carry it out. It was a familiar feeling – each of her previous babies had engendered it in her as well. But it had seemed to have meaning then, whereas now it felt pointless.

She had no appetite – everything felt wrong. Part of it was due to the heat. Visitors to the area often dismissed it as a "dry" heat, but 110 degrees was 110 degrees, no matter the humidity. It sapped Domer's strength until she felt like a wet rag. Her normally vibrant hair had lost its luster, clumping about her shoulders.

But the real reason she felt wrong was because the *baby* felt wrong. Domer couldn't shake the premonition she'd had a few weeks earlier. It had been like a knife in her guts and it had terrified her. But she had refused to dwell on it or even mention it to Will. He was worried enough about her already.

The baby moved - surprisingly it relieved some pressure. Temporarily she felt a little better.

But it didn't last long. "You'd better git Will back in here."

Mary dispatched her seven year-old granddaughter, Lucy, to find him.

Pain wracked Domer's body then. A deep-down, monstrous thing. It left further weakness in its wake.

Will returned with an anxious look on his face. "How's she doin', ma?" he asked as he sat beside his wife.

"As well as kin be 'spected at this point," was all she replied.

The knife came back suddenly to Domer and with it the icy-chill of a mother's certainty that something was very wrong. It tore at her heart. Although she tried to keep it off her face, she knew it was too late – he had always been able to read her like a book. Concern and worry was written in every blink of his eyes. Those green eyes she adored.

The baby was coming too soon. And it was coming the wrong way. She knew it. At 41, she had already given birth to eleven children and knew what to expect. This wasn't it. Always smooth during pregnancy, each birth had also been relatively easy. But this one had been different from the start and was not going smoothly at all.

Still a strikingly handsome, dark-haired beauty, she'd never been able to keep anything from her husband of 24 years.

As she looked at him she was suddenly taken back to when she'd first seen those eyes. She'd been only 12 years old - he was sitting there fully clothed in the middle of that natural pond underneath the huge cottonwood tree in Arizona with a ridiculous grin on his face; as if he'd decided for himself it was the best place to dismount.

Ripples from the shock were still receding when he had turned and looked straight into her, smiling and unconcerned, perhaps a little surprised to find her and the others watching him, but, as always, in command of the situation no matter how funny or serious it might be.

Those same eyes looked at her now, tempered by age. Laugh lines that were evidence of an indomitably cheery spirit in the face of life-long toil and hardship, now were changed to worry about something he could not control.

One hand on her stomach and the other stroking her sweat-damp hair both communicated his concern for her. Against this he could not protect her.

He looked at his mother again, midwife to hundreds of successful deliveries, and saw his worry reflected in her face.

The baby kicked feebly once more - Domer squinted and caught her breath. Feet were in the wrong place, coming first.

Her eyes met his again and in that shared eternal moment they both knew.

"Will, I'm gonna need some hot water an' towels," Mary said quietly.

"I'll git Lucy ta bring some."

"No. I need *you* ta go git 'em." She looked at him pointedly.

Will rose slowly with a nod, giving Domer a reassuring smile he did not feel. He trudged out of their little bedroom feeling lost with worry, never noticing the neat stack of folded towels sitting next to the steaming pan of water.

Mary closed the door softly behind him.

Columbus, New Mexico - July 2 - 3:47am

Domer Edith Parks woke to the jarring sound of pounding on her front door.

What on earth...? she thought. She found her brother Lorin there, hat in hands, lathered horse behind him with head hanging, reins dangling free, forgotten. Lorin's expression was indescribably sad. A chill swept over her.

"What's happened? Come in, Lorin, an' tell me what's wrong." Her world tilted. *It's gotta be ma or pa.*

They sat at the small kitchen table. "Waal, it's ma...she...she's..." He couldn't go on. The silence lasted forever.

Ma. She was pregnant. This was about her time...

"An' the baby?" she whispered, her throat constricted, mouth suddenly dry.

Lorin shook his head, unable to meet her eyes.

"When...?"

"Las' evenin' 'round 5 or so. I come fer ya fast as I could. Switched horses twice."

She looked at the clock. *Ten or 'leven hours. He mus' have ridden like a madman.* "Why din't ya send a telegraph?"

"Red-Flaggers cut the lines at Ascención an' it musta shorted out in Díaz too. When they git it fixed they'll let Bill 'n RJ know. They're over ta the RO headquarters, 'posedly, wranglin' critters an' keepin' peace at the mines. Fay'n the rest a the younger ones'r heppin' down home."

Edith's mind went into high gear. She would have to grieve later. There would be plenty of time for that. Now was the time of doing.

"An' pa? How's he holdin' up?"

"He was jes sittin' thar in the front room. Not sayin' much. Grandma was thar too – she been kinder takin' care a things."

She got up hastily. "I've gotta go. He needs me down there now. Grandma too. You kin take Stinker back with ya – lead yer tired out hoss. I'll follow 'long quick as I can."

"Ya got another hoss 'sides Stinker ta pull yer buckboard?"

"No, but I'll borra one. Now git! Don't kill them animals, but tell 'em I'll be thar as soon's I can. 'Specially tell pa an' Bishop Davis."

"A'right." Lorin was one year older than his sister, but she'd always had a way about her that was like their father. People looked to her as a natural leader.

Her husband, Charlie Parks, had come into the room still sleepy and hair mussed. Lorin nodded to him and left.

"What's goin' on? It's practically the middle a the night..."

"Ma died last night. I gotta go down ta Díaz," she said simply.

"Aw no, darlin'! I'm so sorry ta hear it! 'Course ya gotta go. Now le's fig're how's the bes' way. What 'bout Arthur an' thet fancy car a his?"

After some further discussion they agreed a car would be the quickest method of getting to Díaz. Their neighbor and friend, Arthur Evans, was soon roused from his slumber and hired to drive his two year-old Stanley Steamer as transport. Charlie caught Lorin before he left on Stinker and instead both siblings ended up traveling the 60 miles into Mexico together by steam automobile.

◆

It took almost an hour for the party of three to start out. First, Evans had to get out of bed and dressed. Then, while the boiler warmed, he topped off the gasoline and kerosene mixture of fuel the car took, as well as filled the water tank to the brim. Fortunately, he had left the pilot lit the previous evening so the two main burners came right on. The Stanley Model 70 Touring Car had a rear seat into which Evans put several extra water cans and one spare can of fuel. There was still room for Lorin, but just barely.

They stopped at the border station where two rough-looking Mexican officials in dirty, faded uniforms with red ribbons tied in their button holes asked them their business in Mexico. Edith and Lorin spoke fluent Spanish, but the driver Evans not a word.

Edith acted as translator.

"Mi madre murió ayer y hay que dar prisa para ayudar con los arreglos."

(My mother died yesterday and we must hurry to help with the arrangements.)

The leader took off his sweat-stained hat with a flourish and held it over his heart, a look of genuine concern on his face. His younger companion did the same. At 5 in the morning, these were not the brightest of officials, but they were polite to a fault.

"Oh, lo siento mucho, señorita. ¿Cuanto tiempo va a estár en México?"

(Oh, I'm so sorry, miss. How long will you be in Mexico?)

"Pocos días para ayudar a mi padre a través de este difícil momento."

(Just a few days to help my father through this difficult time.)

"Eso está muy bien. Por favór proceda rápidamente y vaya con Dios."

(That's fine. Please proceed quickly and go with God.)

"Gracias, jefe. Es ustéd muy amable."

(Thank you, sir. You are very kind.)

It couldn't hurt to butter up this lowly border worker with a little extra respect, she thought. After all, he hadn't even asked for the normal bribes, which was how they made their pittance of a living. He'd probably be called to account later by his immediate boss, but that wasn't her concern.

They all noticed the ribbons tied to the buttons - the Red-Flaggers were in charge of the border today.

"Go ahead, Arthur. We're cleared."

Evans looked amazed. "Really? I rather expected they'd extract quite a large bribe for letting the car go in!" he said as he pushed up the throttle lever on the steering column.

"Please jes go 'fore they change their mind," she said under her breath.

As soon as they hit the main road Evans pushed the car to as fast as 25 miles per hour where he could without hurting his precious Stanley. It was capable of going much faster, but on that road 25 was about the best they could do safely. Frequently they had to slow down to 15 or even 10 miles per hour - sometimes they had to crawl over bad patches.

The trip took them a little over four hours. They stopped to fill up the fuel once and the water tank twice. Miracle of miracles was they didn't have to change even one tire. They arrived at 9:27 in the morning.

Colonia Díaz - 9:35am

"Bishop took yer ma over ta the church. Sisters is dressin' her up nice an' Rasmus Larsen is busy makin' the coffin."

Her father looked like hell warmed over. His eyes were expressionless and, what worried her more, vacant. Edith hoped his incredible vitality was merely hibernating rather than extinguished.

"Pa, ya need ta sit down," she said, hugging him. "Ya look like yer gonna tip over."

He sat heavily, his face ashen.

Mary bustled into the house - the two Adams women exchanged another embrace.

"I'm so sorry 'bout yer ma, chil'. We tried ever'thin' we could think a, but nuthin' hepped. Nuthin'. She jes slid down 'til it was a mercy she went through. I was at muh wits ends. Onny God knows His ways. He musta needed her early is all I kin fig're."

Edith thought she looked haggard. *Poor woman. She did all she could an' it wasn't enough.*

"Grandma, as hard as it is, we can't do nuthin' but our best an' let God take care a the rest.

Mary sighed. "Bless ya, chil' fer comin' so quick. Now we gotta go on takin' care a the

267

livin'," she said, stealing a worried glance at her son.

Evans stuck his head in the door at that point. "Pardon me for intruding, but I think I'll be on my way back to Columbus now, unless you think you might have need of the car again."

"No, Arthur you've been a dear. You go on home an' take care. Tell Charles fer me thet I'll be back in a few days, would ya?"

"Yes, I will do that. My deepest condolences again to you, Mr. Adams." Evans stuck out his hand but Will didn't notice – he was far away, deep in memories.

Edith jumped up to give him a hug. "Thank ya again, Arthur. I don't know what I'd've done without ya."

"Nonsense. Happy to help." They both looked at Will.

"Well, I'll be on my way, then." He left and soon they heard the unmistakable whooshing sound of the steam engine fading away.

"He's a nice boy," Mary said.

Edith nodded.

They all sat together then, in silence, each alone with their thoughts. The hours passed slowly that way, the sounds of children at play outside the only reminder that life was still going on.

At length, Will left to be with his wife.

2:53pm

"Will, I wonder if I might have a minute." Brady Davis knew he had to be careful with his old friend.

He nodded without emotion. "Shore, Bishop."

They exited the church where the bodies were being prepared and stood under the shade of a cottonwood. Will was glad to be away from the ghastly sight and nauseating carbolic fumes. His wife's remains were lying on a board suspended between two chairs with a heavy Bible on her stomach and the tiny baby on her chest. Women had been preparing the bodies and preserving

269

them as best they could by covering them with a sheet and cloths drenched with salt peter and carbolic-acid water. Domer and the baby would be buried together.

"It's been an awful day. I haven't been able to tell you properly yet how sorry I am for your loss."

Will gazed at the horizon and didn't reply. He was still far away.

"We should be able to start the service in a few hours when it's cooler. Does six o'clock suit you?"

"Thet's fine."

"I'm glad to see Edith here. Lorin made quite a ride to bring her down. I'm only sorry we couldn't get in touch with Bill and Roy. The lines are fixed up now, but in this heat there's no possibility of waiting for them even if we had been able to send a telegraph right off."

"Thet's jes the way it is."

"Yes, very unfortunate indeed." He hesitated before going on. "There's one other thing. I hate to bring it up at all, but some of the women were a

270

bit uncomfortable with you wearing your guns inside the church. I assured them you meant no disrespect."

Will looked at his long-time friend evenly, eyes coming back to the present-day. He unconsciously felt the ubiquitous Colts at his sides. After gathering his thoughts he spoke quietly.

"Waal, Bishop, ya kin jes tell 'em I won't be bringin' no guns ta the service. With things the way they are 'round here these days, ya'd think them wimmen'd be happy ta see a few armed men. But I'm a-gonna tell ya sumthin' - right 'bout now guns're the las' thing on muh mind."

"Of course. I'm sorry for mentioning such a silly thing, Will. You come to the church any way you like." He felt small beside the man's grief and obvious pain.

No more words passed between them for some minutes. A lone dove called at regular intervals from the branches above.

When Will spoke again it was as if to someone far away, voice quiet and composed – eyes misted over with distance, searching the northern horizon.

"If'n ya wanna, ya might do me a favor, Brady."

"Anything, Will. You just name it."

Will did.

Davis was surprised and a little ashamed he hadn't thought of it himself. "Absolutely, I'll take care of that for you," he said.

Imperceptibly Will nodded and then resolutely walked off alone up the dusty street.

Brady watched his old friend go and was suddenly overcome with sadness – for Will, for his family, for Colonia Díaz and the people - his people for so much of his life. He shook his head, trying to throw out the darkness, yet the small but persistent voice inside whispered forebodings to his troubled mind. He had little idea where to turn or what to do. Then the answer occurred to him - as it always had in good times or bad - he'd retire to pray his supplications to the Almighty at the soonest opportunity.

But first he had something to do. He disconsolately trudged off in the direction of the Telegraph office hoping he could send a special message now that the lines had been fixed.

3:15pm

Edith had taken it on herself to get her younger siblings bathed and their Sunday best clothes laid out and pressed. In a family of boys, she was the woman of the house now. She couldn't believe her mother was gone. Domer had always been her rock.

Enough a that, she thought. *This ain't the time. Concentrate.*

But, oh mama! What's pa ever gonna do without you? He looks so lost now.

Will walked into the house, saying nothing. He went into the bedroom and closed the door.

Lorin came in soon after, dressed in his cowboy-finest. Edith noticed his boots had been shined.

"Rest a the kids gettin' ready?" he asked.

"They are. Ya look nice."

"Thanks."

He leaned against the wall and studied her. "Ya doin' a'right?"

"I s'pose so. I'm worried 'bout pa, though. He hardly speaks."

"He's half dead 'thout ma. They been two beans in a pod fer so long now. I shore miss 'er already. Jes don' hardly seem real." Lorin's voice had grown husky.

Edith looked away. "Somehow it seems a end ta things. What with all the revolution an' counter-revolution an' now ma gone – nothin's ever gonna be the same. I might have ta take Lucy an' Thad an' Karl an' Lloyd back with me. Dangerous down here these days."

"It's them Red-Flaggers mostly," Lorin replied. "But ya never know who's in charge from one day ta the next. An' they all switch sides at the drop of a hat. Whoever's winnin' is who they'll all jump in with."

"Such a shame there's so little loyalty. It's impossible ta fig're what might be comin' next. Thet's why it's so dangerous."

"Yep. Dangerous," said their father from the doorway, startling them. "We'll talk 'bout all thet later," he said.

He was dressed in his black, broad-cloth suit. Conspicuous by their absence were his guns. Lorin and Edith noticed immediately.

"Pa, I don't think I seen ya with no gun belt on mebbe twice in my life," Lorin observed.

"Some a them ladies down ta the church thought it un-proper bringin' in guns, so I left 'em off. I'll not have one ounce a disrespect shown yer ma by anyone. Nor any whispers, neither." His face made chiseled granite look soft.

Edith shivered despite herself. She was used to his iron personality, but this was harder than she'd ever known him. *He's holdin' it all inside so tight*, she thought to herself. *I hope he doesn't break.*

275

3:43pm

A thunder of hooves and cloud of dust in the street announced trouble.

"*¿Donde está la señora Parks?*" came an angry voice, confirming it.

(Where is Mrs. Parks?)

Will, Lorin and Edith went outside, standing by the white picket fence.

The speaker was a burly man with a huge, round sombrero and drooping mustache. He was obviously the leader of the six men. The officials were all armed and had red ribbons tied to their saddles. The mood was ominous.

"*Estóy Edith Parks. ¿Hay algún problema, oficial?*"

(I'm Edith Parks. Is there some trouble, officer?)

"*¿Eres ustéd la que vino en el coche de Columbus?*"

(Are you the one who came in the car from Columbus?)

276

"Sí, mi amigo me llevó en su coche para que yo pudiera ayudar con el funerál de mi madre. Murió ayer."

(Yes, my friend brought me in his car so that I could help with my mother's funeral. She died yesterday.)

"Lo siento por eso. ¿Donde está el coche y su amigo ahora? No llenó los papeles nesesarios y no pagó el peaje para traer un coche en México."

(I'm sorry about that. Where is the car and your friend now? He didn't fill out the right papers and pay the toll for bringing a car into Mexico.)

"Regresó a los Estados Unidos hace un par de horas."

(He went back to the United States a few hours ago.)

She prayed silently Arthur had made it back across the border safely.

Immediately his temper soared. *"Ustéd lo debe traer él de vuelta o pagar el peaje y una multa a ti mismo! Vamos a arrestár a ustéd hasta que se pague el monto totál para nosotros."*

277

(You must bring him back or pay the toll and a fine yourself! We will have to arrest you until the full amount is paid to us.)

Will spoke up quickly, trying to defuse the situation. *"Espera, espera, oficial. Podemos resolvér esto. ¿Cuánto necesita?"*

(Wait, wait, officer. We can work this out. How much do you require?)

"¿Y quién es ustéd?" he spat contemptuously at Will.

(And just who are you?)

"Soy padre de ella, Will Adams. Estóy seguro de que podemos resolvér esto a su satisfacción."

(I'm her father, Will Adams. I'm sure we can work this out to your satisfaction.)

"Todos ustedes capitalistas norteamericanos. Creen que pueden hacer lo que quieren hacer y salen con la suya. Le digo que la hora viene cuando vamos a recuperar toda esta tierra de los gringos en el nombre de las personas que ustedes han robado! Ustedes no deben de estár aquí!"

He gestured wildly around him.

(All you capitalistic Americans. You think you can do anything you want and get away with it. I tell you the time is coming when we will take back all this land from the gringos in the name of the people you have stolen it from! You should not be here!)

Several horses stamped nervously at this vehement outburst and a few of his own men glanced at him.

This was getting out of hand quickly. Will wondered how to placate the irate official and suddenly felt very vulnerable without his guns.

One of his men leaned over and whispered something in his leader's ear, indicating Will. The Mexican grew more cautious and calculating.

"¿Ustéd es él que llaman 'Dos-Pistolas'?"

(You are the one they call 'Two-Gun'?)

Will sighed. He felt very tired of such a triviality. *"Sí, algunos así me llaman. ¿Por favor, cuanto es la multa?"*

(Yes, some do. How much is the fine?)

"He oído que ha matado más que veinte hombres y siempre tienen sus armas puestas. ¿Dónde están?"

(I heard you have killed more than 20 men and always have your guns on. Where are they?)

"No necesito unas armas para el funerál de mi esposa, y ahora estamos tarde para eso."

(I don't need a gun for my wife's funeral, which we are now late for.)

Immediately the Mexican drew his own gun to cover Will. His men followed suit, several clearly not understanding why they were threatening these unarmed people.

"Ustéd no va a ninguna parte! Ahora ustéd no es un hombre tan grande, sin sus armas, ¿Eh?" he laughed.

(You're not going anywhere! Now you are not such a big man without your guns, huh?)

He cocked his pistol, aimed straight at Will's face from less than ten feet away. Will stood solid as the hills - unarmed, but unafraid, staring down the maw of evil and hatred with unflinching bravery. Not a word did he offer. Tension hung palpably. Another horse grew skittish, tossing its head and snorting.

"*Bueno, gringo? ¿Qué tienes que decír ahora?*"

(Well, gringo? What have you to say now?)

No reply.

"*¿Qué tal te pongas de rodillas para suplicár por su vida, arrogante hijo - - - - - -!*"

(How about you get on your knees to beg for your life, you arrogant son - - - - - - - - !)

Will didn't move an inch – he simply waited, regarding the Mexican as a mountain lion would a coiled rattlesnake.

"*Por Dios, a todos los gringos deben aprender una lección!*"

(By God, all you damn gringos should be taught a lesson!)

Edith, sensing disaster, stepped in front of her implacable father with her hands in a calming attitude, thinking no one would shoot their gun towards a woman.

She was mistaken.

Two shots rang out in quick succession - the murderous Red-Flagger and one of his men had both fired. Edith felt one bullet part her hair - she crouched involuntarily. The other plowed harmlessly into the dirt at her feet. Turning, she saw her father holding his bleeding neck, gaze locked on the Mexican, still rooted in place.

"Vamos, muchachos!" the Mexican screamed with a toothy sneer at Will. *"Hemos enseñado a los gringos suficiente por hoy! Pero nos volveremos a deshacerse de todo lo que la gente maldita blancos fuera de México! Sólo espera y verás!"*

(Let's go, boys! We've taught the gringos enough for today! But we'll be coming back to get rid of all you damn white people out of Mexico! Just you wait and see!)

Wheeling their horses in confusion, they galloped off south towards La Ascención, red ribbons flying. The dust cleared and one remained behind, siting atop his horse, looking sadly down at Edith and her father.

"Lo siento por eso. Él no habla por todos nosotros aquí en México." He tipped his sombrero and with a sympathetic look on his face rode slowly away.

(I'm sorry about that. He doesn't speak for all of us here in Mexico.)

In shock, Lorin stepped in to catch his father as he finally moved, taking a step and then collapsing. Edith fell to her knees, trying in vain to stem the flow from the mortal wound.

Will focused on their stricken faces as the clock of his life wound down. "Be good an' take care a each other. RJ, ya hurry 'long an' git yer ma...." He appeared confused looking at Lorin and then lost his thought.

His intensely green eyes cleared for a moment and he smiled at something far distant only he could see. "Shoulda listened better ta 'Ol Port," he said wryly. "Tell Edge I...." He was taken then by a violent fit of coughing, his life's last blood seeping fast into the thirsty ground. His eyes closed and a calm look came over his entire countenance.

283

Thirteen year-old Alvin Larsen, there to inform Mr. Adams that his wife's coffin was ready, had hidden across the street in some bushes, riveted all throughout to the scene with terrified fascination. He fled back to his father's shop bearing the horrible news, thinking any moment the *bandidos* might come back and shoot him too.

Whatever else Will Adams had thought of saying to his long-absent older brother would never be known for he died then and there in his son's arms, Edith weeping over him and praying silently.

5:15pm

The mood in Díaz was somber and unbelieving. Almost unnoticed, ominously dark thunderheads had boiled out of the west with singular rapidity, towering to incredible heights over much of northern Mexico.

Another casket had been ordered from Rasmus Larsen. The women who prepared Domer's body now did the same for Will through tears of sadness and fear of what the future might hold.

Later, other women stood a macabre vigil overnight in turns, keeping mice and feral cats away from the corpses as rain drummed the church roof, softened the caliche and cleansed the blood-soaked earth.

July 3

At 10:00am Bishop Brady Davis conducted the triple funeral service. The church was packed to overflowing with colonists from miles around, the women wielding fans against the already stifling heat. Many local Mexican friends came to pay their last respects too. Everyone knew Will and Domer – and they were well-liked.

285

Afterward, while taking stock of their grim situation in small groups of determined men, now armed to the teeth, the refrain most often heard was "If they can murder Will Adams, they can murder any of us."

There were rumors of fifty Red-Flaggers on their way from La Ascención intent on wiping out the rest of them. The men of Díaz resolved themselves to a different result.

A pall had fallen over Díaz which then spread throughout the colonies in Mexico. Common expectations were of further horrors to come.

And they were right.

July 5

Brady Davis had trouble focusing on the blurry words he was trying to write. He had no idea if his several unanswered telegraphs were getting through, but it was the least he could do to keep trying since it was the last thing Will ever asked of him.

He couldn't believe they were really gone. Will had been the underpinning of most any bit of protection felt in Díaz. Now all that had vanished in the blink of an eye. He wondered if the Lord was testing them – for so long so many had relied on Will to be their security blanket.

Now it was time they stood together and took matters into their own hands. He vowed one way or another they would no longer be as sheep offered up for the slaughter.

He took a deep breath and finished writing out the bad news again.

La Ascención - July 12

Davis sat alone watching as General Juarez rode into the town square with 25 seasoned *Federales* at his back. The spectacle was more than a little intimidating. A few days earlier he'd been summoned, not asked, to a special meeting with the General.

Juarez dismounted and removed his immaculate white gloves. His men spread out through the square, vigilant eyes roaming over the locals, sword hilts gleaming in the sun.

He stood, hat in hand, as the General and a captain stepped onto the low porch fronting the adobe structure which served as the magistrate's office and jail.

The General was not smiling.

"El señor Davis, ¿Verdad? Desde Colonia Díaz?"

(Mr. Davis, is it? From Colonia Díaz?)

"Sí, generál, es un gran privilegio para reunirse con ustéd hoy aquí," Davis replied, offering his hand.

(Yes, General, it is a great privilege to meet with you here today.)

Juarez shook his hand and sat. *"Su español es muy bueno. ¿Dónde aprendiste a hablar como un nativo?"*

(Your Spanish is very good. Where did you learn to speak as a native?)

"De mis muchos años viviendo aquí en las colonias, Excelencia."

(From my many years living here in the colonies, Excellency.)

Juarez looked impatient. *"Voy a ser breve. Los Banderas-Colorados son más que campesinos molestos con horcas. Pronto tendremos el contról de todo el distrito. Pronto ustéd no tendrá nada que temer de ellos pronto."*

(I'll be brief. The Red-Flaggers are nothing but annoying peasants with pitchforks. We will soon control the entire district and you will have nothing to fear from them.)

"Con el perdón de muestra Excelencia, pero tienen muchas armas y ellos son más que una molestia. Varios de mis personas fueron asesinados."

(Begging your Excellency's pardon, but they have many guns and they are more than just an annoyance. Several of my people have been killed.)

The general considered. *"Sea como fuere, se requiere que los colonos de Díaz a entregar todas las armas a mi ejército en una semana."*

(Be that as it may, the colonists at Díaz are required to hand over all weapons to my army in one week.)

"Pero el generál, si nos entregamos nuestras armas a cualquiera que no vamos a tener una manera de proteger a nuestros hogares y familias ..."

(But General, if we turn over our weapons to anyone we won't have a way to protect our homes and families...)

Juarez waved away the objection as if it were a fly. *"Es de ninguna consecuencia - te protegeremos. En una semana tendré Capitán Silva llevar a sus hombres a recogerlos. Las municiones también."*

(It is of no consequence – we will protect you. In a weeks time I will have Captain Silva bring his men to collect them. Ammunition too.)

Davis was panicked but tried not to let it show. *"Excelencia, lo que pides es un suicidio para la Colonia Díaz. Por favor, les pido que lo reconsideré."*

(Excellency, what you ask is suicide for Colonia Díaz. Please, I beg you to reconsider.)

He rose forcing Davis to stand as well.

"La decisión ya ha sido tomada. Voy a enviar representantes a las otras colonias para hacerles saber las órdenes, también. Una semana más, Sr. Davis. Entonces mis hombres vienen para las armas y municiones los qual su gente tienen."

(The decision has already been made. I will send representatives to the other colonies to let them know the orders, as well. One week, Mr. Davis. Then will my men come for the guns and ammunition your people have.)

Turning his back on Davis he commanded Silva: *"Capitán! Traiga mi caballo y reunír a los hombres. Vamos!"*

(Captain! Bring my horse and gather the men. We go!)

Brady Davis felt helpless as he watched them ride away. It was the end. Defenseless without weapons, a repeat on a much larger scale of the murder of Will Adams was not only probable, it seemed inevitable. He remembered what he'd told himself just a few days earlier. No more sheep.

There could be no option now other than to abandon what they had built in the colonies. At least for a while. When events cooled, perhaps they could come back to their homes and rebuild their lives. Time would tell.

He felt the eyes of all La Ascención on him as he rode back to Díaz that day. It was as if they knew that soon there would be plunder for the taking just a few miles north.

The final back-breaking straw had been loaded by General Juarez. Without some miraculous intervention, the Mormon exodus from Mexico would begin within days.

◆

292

The telegraphs had been delivered. Almost a thousand miles away, a face etched by the passing of 62 out-of-doors years wore a grim expression as the man it belonged to wrote out his reply.

His well-worn Colt was tied down, every loop in his gun belt filled. His horse waited restlessly - traveling bags over its withers, bedroll tied up behind with a loaded Winchester in the saddle boot.

Done writing, he placed a silver dollar on top of the form and walked out without a word, not waiting for a confirmation or change.

Uh oh, the operator thought after reading over the form, shaking his head. *Somebody better be lookin' to their hole card when* that *cowboy shows up.*

He consulted his book for the destination station number, noted the time and tapped out the short message:

To: Brady Davis
Colonia Diaz, Mexico

From: Edge Bellows
CE Ranch, Nevada, USA

Sent: 7,12,1912 8:25a

Message:
Hold All Guilty Persons STOP
On My Way STOP

END

After July, 1912

Two-Gun is an historical novel based on true stories and real people. Some of the events and characters were made up or embellished to help support the main story line, but all of the basic history, people, dates and places are as true and accurate as is possible given sometimes conflicting accounts of the same events (especially the Civil War), not to mention the error-inducing necessity of writing at several removes from the events themselves. The central characters were real and actually did most of the things I wrote about them doing.

◆

The Colt Single Action Army, or "Peacemaker", as it was nicknamed, was uniquely suited to the era in which it was used.

In my opinion, it was truly one of the guns that helped tame the west, another being the 1873 Winchester lever action rifle.

There is no doubt in my mind that Will's skill with such guns, honed on a daily basis by practicing and using them from an early age, would equal or exceed today's best shooters. And that skill helped bring stability and safety to a world more often than not otherwise overrun with injustice and danger.

◆

In the United States at that time it was taken for granted that the second amendment to the Constitution meant Americans would be free to keep and bear arms in their own defense, if needed. However, that meant nothing in Mexico, which did not have then, nor has had since, any such similar codified freedom for the people.

It is interesting and sobering to note that the final cause for the colonists to abandon Mexico over 100 years ago was when their ability for self-defense was confiscated from them by the government and *bandidos* under whose control they found themselves.

Fortunately, they had somewhere to go, where the freedom to defend oneself, family and property was the accepted way of life. But even more – to do otherwise was unthinkable and cowardly.

◆

No one knows what happened to Will's Frontier Peacemakers after he took them off for the last time to attend his wife's funeral. We only know he never put them on again.

It's possible, but unlikely, they were handed over to the Mexican Army or the Red-Flaggers along with some of the other guns the Mormons had in the colonies. If that happened someone may still have one or both and maybe even Will's gun belt. More likely is they were rushed out to the Corner Ranch in a wagon-load of other guns the colonists didn't want to give up. Sadly, it's probable they all have been lost to history and those turbulent revolutionary times.

◆

Speaking of when Will was killed, Annie Johnson, author of the great book *Heartbeats of Colonia Díaz*, writes: "... was a sad day for all of Díaz as they buried Brother and Sister Adams side by side in the Díaz cemetery, but especially so for the eight orphaned children, of whom Edyth (sic) was the only one married."

With all due respect, this sentiment, while touching, is perhaps not quite indicative of the true characters of the sons and daughters Will and Domer left behind. Almost every one of the boys was a superb cowboy and rugged individual.

My great grandfather, Roy Jefferson (or RJ or simply "Pop" as he was called) got mad at being beaten with a ruler for using his left hand at school (among other reasons) and left home from Díaz when he was 14 years old to go cowboying in other parts of northern Mexico for Colonel Greene on the massive RO ranch.

William Adams, Junior (Uncle Bill) was banned along with brothers Lorin and Fay from local rodeos because if they entered no one else could win. Fay was later a world champion calf roper and is shown horseback in a picture shaking hands with Will Rogers in New York.

Edith, who had come home for her mother's funeral, stepped in front of her unarmed father, Will, thinking to protect *him* from the *bandido* Red-Flaggers. The bullet passed over her head and through the jugular vein of Will. He then took a few steps bleeding profusely, fell into his son Lorin's arms, and died. Edith was 19 and Lorin 20 at the time. Not a shrinking violet among them.

◆

It has been advanced by some scholars that Pancho Villa helped drive the Mormons out of Mexico, but that simply isn't the case. For one thing, he had been in jail for some while before and during the time of the exodus. For another, it has been well documented the colonists and Villa were usually on good terms. Villa knew them as hard-working, honest people and for the most part left them alone.

Some of his men and other revolutionaries, as well as many of the Federal troops and later the Red-Flaggers were a different story. The sentiment against capitalistic Americans in Mexico at that time ran high, the flames fanned by communist-backed organizers of mine workers.

The meeting on Richin's ranch between Villa and the fictional Bishop Brady Davis (it was actually Bishop Johnson there that day) might very likely have taken place almost exactly as written. Respect was mutual.

My own great-grandfather on my grandmother's side talks in the book *The Life and Times of Harvey Hyrum Taylor* about feeding both the *Federales* and the revolutionaries in turn. They had to get along with both sides, and, pretty much, they did.

◆

Most of the colonists who fled never returned exept for the occasional visit. I can remember taking trips to Mexico as a young boy to visit the colonies. My grandfather and father would point out different features unique to those places, but the one that stuck with me was the abundant deep, wide canals the colonists built and used to irrigate the otherwise bleak desert landscape. A few were still sparsely used, but most were dry and had long before fallen into sad disrepair.

After the colonists left, many of their homes were torn apart by the local Mexican population looking for the gold they thought must be hidden in the walls. The colonists had worked so hard and became so prosperous, some of the Mexican people just assumed they must be mining gold somewhere in the mountains and hoarding it.

Beautiful homes, situated along straight, broad, tree-lined streets were ripped apart rather than occupied. Practically all of Colonia Díaz was burned. Ironically, Will and Domer's house survived into the 1950's.

Today almost nothing exists of the thriving communities the Mormon colonists built in Mexico.

Brigham City is a ghost town now but you can yet see remnants of those long walls JJ built his home inside of.

Woodruff is still a tiny community on the Little Colorado.

Of Wilford, founded by JJ in 1883, nothing remains but whispers through the trees. The Aztec cowboys permanently wiped it out.

◆

Our family has in its possession the headstone from the grave of JJ. How we got it is a whole other story, which is not necessarily all completely within the letter of the law, Mexican or American. On this headstone is a carved picture of a hand rising from the dust, holding an open *Book of Mormon*.

How this man got from Sidney, Iowa to Salt Lake City with the intention of hanging Brigham Young, and then dying in Mexico while residing with and helping protect his polygamist friends, to finally having his last sentiments expressed on his headstone that way, is a testimony in itself.

We should get to know our ancestors. I believe they know us. They watch and see what we do with their names and the legacies they left us. Many of them accomplished astounding things.

If we forget, how can we in turn expect but to be forgotten?

◆

Henry 1583-1646
Henry 1610-1676
Moses 1654-1724
James 1693-1727
James 1722-1755
Samuel 1752-1838
John 1779-1851
William Jefferson 1812-1888
Jerome Jefferson 1835-1902
William (Will) 1859-1912
Roy Jefferson 1895-1959
Willie Roy 1919-
William Floyde 1940-
William Lee 1962-
Elise Noelle 1986-
Nolan Floyde 1988-
Justina Lee 1990-
William Logan 1995-

PICTURES

Jerome Jefferson Adams

Will Adams

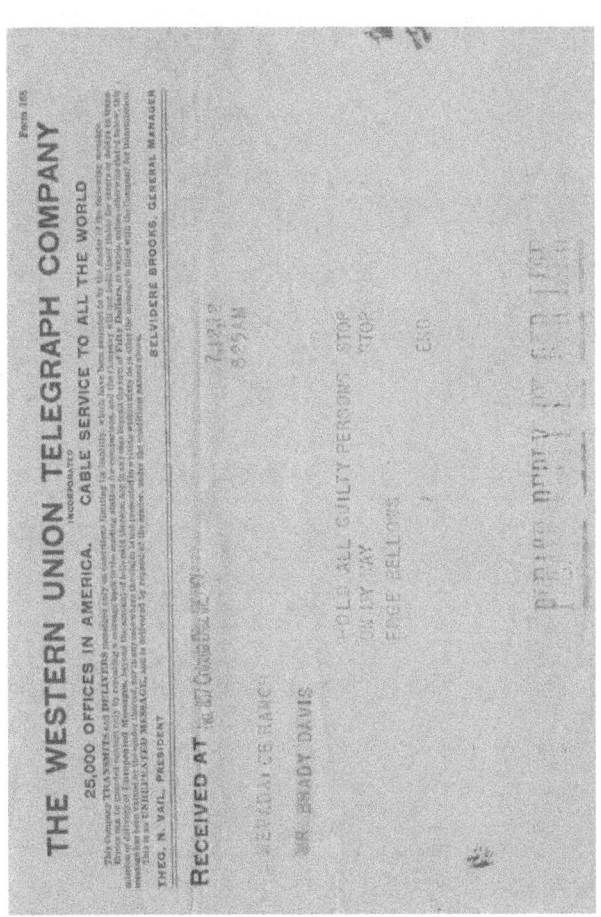

Telegraph Reply From Edge Bellows

JJ's Headstone

Acknowledgments

Putting together even a modest book like this takes a *lot* of help. I'd like to thank a few people who did:

Of course, my parents lent moral support all along the way and encouraged me to keep going. My dad especially never tired of re-hashing the old stories for me and clearing up details. He also made sure the Spanish was correct. He is fluent.

My uncle Bob took time from his incredibly busy schedule to struggle through the raw text of each section. He returned corrections usually in a day - sometimes even within a few hours. He was a big-time cheering section all by himself.

My 95 year-old father-in-law Ted Larsen got a serialized version and never failed to mention how much he liked it. Trying to keep up with his reading kept me at the keyboard or doing research when I might otherwise have slacked off.

My daughter Elise and son Logan helped out with the pictures and graphic design. My son-in-law Joe with the cover painting of Canyon Creek Ranch. My friend Bodie provided the basis and solid character traits of Brady Davis. And master teacher, Inez Alvarez, learnt me spellin' in the seventh grade at Gadsden Junior High despite my best efforts.

All my buds in SASS - Hammer, Henri & Dan, Clark & Annie, Lefty, Doc, Redding & Lil, Rob, Luna, Tex & Cat and all the many others too numerous to mention - and who exemplify the "Cowboy Way" so well - provided inspiration and pieces of characters here and there.

Anyone who lent me their name or part of it I'm glad to know you.

◆

From a fictional standpoint, Gene Rhodes continues to influence and inform my own writing. If an outsider could, in order to gain the most complete understanding of the old west, read but a single "Western" book, he need search no further than Rhodes' masterpiece *Bransford of Rainbow Range (The Little Eohippus)*.

From an historical perspective several works were invaluable to me for research:

To understand what life was like for the colonists in Mexico, *Heartbeats of Colonia Diaz* by Annie R. Johnson and the autobiographical *The Life and Times of Harvey Hyrum Taylor* provided indispensable insight.

For a *gringo* perspective of Mexican Revolutionary times, *Colonel Greene and the Copper Skyrocket* by C.L. Sonnichsen was very well investigated and presented.

The Crooked Trail to Holbrook by Leland J Hanchett, Jr. is a substantive and meticulously researched look into the early cattle industry of Arizona.

In it is the actual history of the Adams ranching influence in Arizona with Will and John Quincy creating the Canyon Creek Ranch just south of the Mogollon Rim in 1883. Today it is known as the OW and is considered by many to be the most beautiful ranch location in Arizona.

Last, but really first, as always, is my own Domer - my wife Chris. The one person without whom I'd seldom have reason to attempt anything worthwhile. Thank you.

◆◆◆